1295

D081070Z

HORACE W. STURGIS
LIBRARY

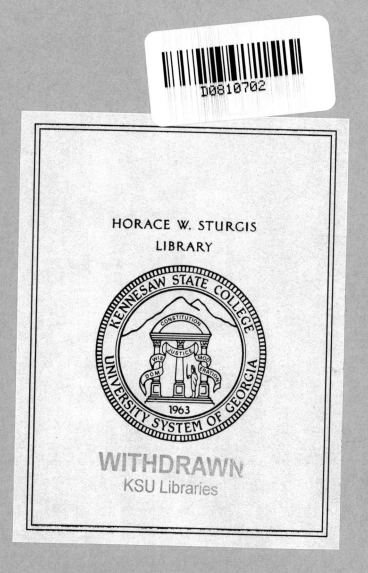

WITHDRAWN
KSU Libraries

In Real Life

In Real Life

J. Hannah Orden

Viking

VIKING
Published by the Penguin Group
Viking Penguin, a division of Penguin Books USA Inc.,
40 West 23rd Street, New York, New York 10010, U.S.A.
Penguin Books Ltd, 27 Wrights Lane, London W8 5TZ, England
Penguin Books Australia Ltd, Ringwood, Victoria, Australia
Penguin Books Canada Ltd, 2801 John Street, Markham, Ontario, Canada L3R 1B4
Penguin Books (N.Z.) Ltd, 182–190 Wairau Road, Auckland 10, New Zealand

Penguin Books Ltd, Registered Offices: Harmondsworth, Middlesex, England

First published in 1990 by Viking Penguin, a division of Penguin Books USA Inc.
1   3   5   7   9   10   8   6   4   2
Copyright © J. Hannah Orden, 1990
All rights reserved

LIBRARY OF CONGRESS CATALOGING IN PUBLICATION DATA
Orden, J. Hannah.   In real life
J. Hannah Orden.   p.   cm.
Summary: Fifteen-year-old Marty meets her first boyfriend at a
park in Brooklyn, but complications arise when she finds herself more
attracted to his best friend.
ISBN 0-670-82679-0
[1. Brooklyn (New York, N.Y.)—Fiction]   I. Title.
PZ7.0627In 1990   [Fic]—dc20   89-22535

Printed in the United States of America
Set in Baskerville

Without limiting the rights under copyright reserved above, no part of this
publication may be reproduced, stored in or introduced into a retrieval system, or
transmitted, in any form or by any means (electronic, mechanical, photocopying, re-
cording or otherwise), without the prior written permission of both the copyright
owner and the above publisher of this book.

To my parents Alex and Susan Orden
for their support in every way

To Susie for her belief and passion
through every draft

And to the young people who inspired this book
for sharing their stories with me

Thank you.

Contents

In Real Life

How Do You Know?

I saw them coming down a little grassy hill in Prospect Park, and I knew I had to follow them. Rap music was blasting out of a giant box they were carrying, and every so often one of them would do a backward flip or another would twirl around. They didn't smile or laugh, but they had a smile in their bodies. When they got to the path, they eased onto it like the merge lane on the expressway and kept moving. There were about eight of them. Teenagers mostly. Maybe a couple in their early twenties. They never spoke to one another, and they never touched, but they moved together to the beat of the music. Like one being.

Everybody who passed turned to look at them. I know because I was skating behind them, and I watched how people reacted. At first they walked by pretending not to notice. But after they passed, they glanced back and, even though most of them probably hate that kind of music and are scared to death of eight black teenagers, at least half of them grinned.

A couple of the guys dropped off to watch some Hare Krishnas. The rest of the group didn't miss a beat. They kept moving. Nobody ever said, "Hey, go on ahead. I want to check this out." They never spoke to one another. There was a club in my school once that was into self-discipline. The members would stand in a row in the cafeteria and stare straight ahead, and if you spoke to them they wouldn't answer you even if they knew you. It was spooky. But the guys I was following weren't spooky like that. They didn't need to talk because they were all part of one being. I was right behind them, so I could see that when those two guys dropped off, the rest of them were uneasy. They didn't look back, but they had to shift their balance the way you would if you lost an arm or a leg.

I was still following them when they left the park and crossed the street. That's when I realized I'd seen them before. There's one corner where they hang out with their friends—girls and guys. I didn't recognize them because they look really different on their corner. As soon as they got there, the silence broke, and they were talking and laughing. I stood across the street and watched them as long as I could without being noticed. That corner was home. It might as well have had their names written on it, and a big brass knocker.

While I was watching, one of the girls started to dance.

She was standing with her girlfriends, but she wasn't talking to them. She was watching the boys and moving to the music. The boys didn't pay any attention to her until she broke away from the girls and danced up to the cutest boy in the whole group. She stood right in front of him and practically rubbed her body against him. Then she turned away and danced back to the girls, looking over her shoulder at that boy. She looked him up and down and nodded, and anyone could tell that she liked what she saw. It was amazing.

The boy acted as if nothing had happened. He kept joking and laughing with his friends. The girl had her back to him, but I knew her back was talking to him, inviting him. I held my breath.

All of a sudden that guy moved. There was a pop and a wave, and he was at her side. Neither of them said a word, but they were dancing together, seducing each other in front of everybody. I couldn't believe it. It was the sexiest thing I had ever seen. Even in the movies.

By the time I left, they'd moved off to the side. That girl was teasing and flirting, and that boy just couldn't keep his hands off her. I didn't know what to think. There's a boy I like who plays baseball in the park. I've never talked to him. But he has blond hair that falls in his eyes, and whenever he goes up to bat, he takes off his cap and pushes his hair back, and I stop breathing. I wish I had the nerve to dance up to him right in the middle of a game and give him a passionate kiss. Of course, he'd lose his head completely and forget all about playing baseball.

I know it shouldn't bother me, but that girl wasn't even pretty. She had gobs of pimples and she's even skinnier than I am. That should be a big relief because I worry about whether anyone will ever want me. Whenever I mention it to Grandma, she jiggles her great big breasts and says, "Don't you worry, Marty—you'll fill out," as if that's a guarantee that someone will love me. But what if it turns out that having someone to love you is not a matter of how pretty you are or whether you've filled out or whether you have a tan? What if it's not any of those things? Then what is it? And how do you know if you've got it?

Coincidences

"We should sell this car and ride the subway," I said. "It's much more reliable."

"Drop it, Marty." Usually Dad has a sense of humor, but that day he lost it when our car died in the middle of Flatbush Avenue. It didn't help that we were taking my grandmother out to celebrate her sixty-seventh birthday. Grandma turned around in the front seat and winked at me. She's always telling Dad to "sell this old junk heap and buy one of those cute little Japanese cars." She didn't say anything this time, but Dad knew what she was thinking.

Dad leaned his head against the steering wheel and waited for the Triple A to come. Grandma's bald boyfriend got out of the car and looked under the hood. It was probably just to impress Grandma, because he's a retired engineer and I think engineers only design things. They don't actually know how they work.

"Maybe the Triple A will come right away." Mom was trying to be helpful, but Dad knows better.

Our car breaks down all the time, and every time the Triple A says it'll have someone there within the hour. But nobody ever comes before the hour's up. Ever. Dad told me that, even if they have nothing better to do, they sit around the garage playing cards until an hour goes by. Then they lean back, stretch, look at the clock on the wall, and say, "Okay, Mike, time to go."

The worst thing was that I was sitting on my mother's lap. I bet Mom liked it because she misses the me that I used to be, and I think she's afraid that she raised a stranger. For one thing, she practically wouldn't recognize me if she bumped into me on the street. I don't let her dress me anymore, and she thinks it's weird what I wear. She says I look as if I am wearing my dad's pajamas and it's not a decent way to go out of the house. She doesn't realize how lucky she is. There's a girl at my school who has a purple Mohawk that sticks straight up in spikes. My hair is still black, the same as ever, and I make it stick up only a little bit. But Mom thinks it's too short. "You looked so pretty with long hair," she says.

The reason I was sitting on my mother's lap is that most of the backseat was filled with helium balloons. When we went to pick up Grandma, a guy in a clown costume pulled up right behind us and delivered an enormous bunch of balloons. Baldy sent them. Grandma shrieked and whooped so everyone in the building could hear, and then she insisted on bringing the balloons with us to the restaurant. Of course, she didn't offer to sit in the backseat with them. And it would never occur to Mom and Dad to ask Baldy to sit in back, even though the balloons were his stupid idea. That's the way it is in our family—the guests always get treated absolutely better than anybody. I wonder if all families are like that. I wonder if there's a family somewhere where the guests get the worst of everything.

If I get married someday and have a family, I'm going to do it differently. When a guest comes over, we'll give him the lumpiest chair that nobody wants and we'll all help ourselves to dinner, and then if there's any left over, he can have some. I suppose we won't have many friends, but that's okay with me because guests are more trouble than they're worth.

Everybody's nice to Baldy because they're so happy Grandma has a boyfriend. I don't understand how anyone who is bald can be a boyfriend, but everyone insists on calling him Grandma's boyfriend. No one has asked for my opinion, but I think Grandma could do much better. I try to keep an open mind, but that day my tolerance was being tested by twelve giant helium balloons.

My worst fear was that a certain boy from the park would pass by and see me. My best friend, Annie, thinks it's stupid to worry about things like that. If she had been there, she would have said that the odds were about a billion to one that he would ride by that spot at that exact time. But much stranger things have happened.

Like that girl who went to Russia and then got killed in a plane crash. The Russians invited her to visit because she was worried about there being a nuclear war. And then what happened to her? She died in an explosion. There was a big flash of light, and—poof!—she was gone. Well, it's spooky, if you ask me. Almost as if she had a premonition that something like this was going to happen to her, but premonitions aren't so specific all the time, so she got mixed up and thought it was a nuclear bomb, when really it turned out to be an airplane crash. She probably should have been writing letters to the Federal Aviation people the whole time instead of the Russians.

I don't care what Annie says, it makes me wonder if there isn't somebody up there arranging these things. In fact, I'm sure there is. Because that boy did ride by on his bicycle. I'd like to know what he was doing on Flatbush Avenue. It's not as if I live in a small town where there's only one main street and anyone who's going anywhere has to go down it. There are lots of other places he could have been on that particular afternoon.

I know I shouldn't waste my time thinking about a boy who doesn't have anything better to do than ride his bike around the city looking for people to embarrass, but I can't help myself. When he rode by, his T-shirt was clinging to his back because he was all sweaty. He'd probably been playing baseball. I skate in the park every day, and I make it a point to swing by the baseball field. He's always there. Besides, that old white

T-shirt was streaked with dirt, as if he'd slid into base. If I hadn't been sitting on my mother's lap, surrounded by balloons, I could have happily died, looking at the way his shirt stuck to his back. But as it was, I glanced at him quickly as I ducked down to fiddle with my shoe.

"Marty," said Mom, "stop squirming."

"My shoe hurts," I said from a safe spot near the floor. I think it was too late, though. I'm sure he saw me.

Lost and Found

Annie insisted I was making a big deal out of nothing. If a boy was riding by on his bicycle in all that traffic, she argued, he wouldn't even have noticed me. She almost had me convinced because I doubt if I'm the kind of person anybody notices.

Then I ran into that boy in the office at school. I was late, and I had to bring in a note. I don't know what he was doing there, but I'm sure he was in trouble. He probably got caught doing something evil and vicious like putting ground glass in the teachers' sandwiches. That's the kind of person I bet he is. Of course, he doesn't look like a mass murderer. He looks more like Hollywood's idea of the perfect teenager. That day in the office he was wearing a school jacket, blue jeans, and hightop sneakers. And maybe I should mention that he's gorgeous. Absolutely, totally gorgeous.

Looks can be deceiving.

When he saw me in the office, he looked me up and down and said, "I've seen you somewhere."

"Probably in the park," I said. "Sometimes I see you playing baseball." The boy kept staring at me, trying to remember. He had that look people get when they're trying to place a name or a face or something. He had nothing better to do since he was going to be in detention for the next five years. If I left quickly, maybe he'd let it slide, but the secretary couldn't find her glasses, which she claimed she needed to read the note I'd brought, so I was stuck there. The boy found what he was looking for before the secretary found her glasses. I knew I was in trouble because a horrible grin spread over his face.

"Oh, yeah. Now I remember. You were in a car. Stuck in the middle of the street."

I glared at him and started reading the bulletin board ferociously. I developed a sudden interest in advanced-placement summer courses at local colleges. *I ought to think about my future,* I told myself, even though I'm only in ninth grade. Finally the secretary found her glasses and wrote me a pass. As I turned to leave, I was sure that boy would say something nasty like, "Do you always sit on your mother's lap?" But the strangest thing happened. He smiled at me and asked me my name.

A Strategy

"Hi, Marty!"

That's all he said: "Hi, Marty!" I was skating down a path in the park, nowhere near the baseball diamond. Of course, I never did dance up to him and seduce him in the middle of a baseball game. I don't know what's wrong with me. When I saw him, my first impulse was to run the other way. I would have, too, except that I knew he'd already seen me, and it would have looked stupid to turn around and skate back the way I'd come.

He was with a friend of his, a guy I'd never seen before. The friend looked older than us, as if he could grow a beard if he wanted to. It made him look kind of raggedy and sexy and definitely cool. He had on one of those black T-shirts with the name of a rock band on it, but it was so faded you couldn't tell anymore what band it was. His blue jeans were worn through at both knees, and he was wearing big work boots laced halfway up and tied around his ankles.

It was a hot day, and the air was so heavy it sank right down between your toes. I knew those big boots couldn't be comfortable. But some people have to look cool no matter how uncomfortable it is. I guess I shouldn't talk since I was wearing roller skates that lace up over my ankles, but at least roller skates serve a purpose. I kind of doubted that this guy was on his way to work at a construction site.

I could think of a few places I would rather have been than roller skating past two guys whose entire purpose in life is to be cool and to make life miserable for anyone who's not. The best I could hope for was that they would ignore me, but as I skated past, the boy who plays baseball reached up, pushed the hair out of his eyes, and said, "Hi, Marty!" I swung around on my skates.

His friend was walking backward, staring at me. I heard him say, "Who is that, Rob?"

Rob didn't turn around, so I couldn't hear what he said. His friend kept walking backward. He looked me right in the eye and whistled. I pivoted and skated away, fast.

According to Annie there is every indication that I have this guy in the palm of my hand.

"Which one?" I asked.

"The baseball player. He's the one you like, ain't he?"

"Yeah." It seemed like a dramatic conclusion to draw

from "Hi, Marty!" "But it was the other one who whistled at me."

"Whistling don't mean nothing. Some guys'll whistle at anything that moves."

I know she's right. Once I saw this woman who was fat, almost as wide as she was tall, dark and sweaty, with a moustache. As I passed, I heard a guy say, "Mmm. Mmm. That's the way I like 'em. Don't give me no skinny broads. Give me a real woman!" But still. I feel just a little bit sexy when a guy whistles at me. I know I shouldn't, but I do.

Annie is not interested in whistlers. She devised a strategy for me. All I have to do for the first three days is skate by the baseball field as if I happened to be passing that way. Then for the next four days I am supposed to stop and watch them play for a few minutes.

Those first two steps don't sound too bad. It's the third part that makes me want to go into deep freeze for a couple of hundred years. At the end of a week, according to Annie, I will be ready to "make my big move." Annie says it doesn't matter how I do it. I can flutter my eyelashes or dance up to him or just ask him to go have an ice cream. My favorite plan is to hunker down behind home plate and get in everybody's way. I love that word—*hunker*. We learned it in English class last year. Finally something I learned in school is going to come in handy. Because I seriously doubt if I am capable of walking up to him straight off and fluttering my eyelashes. And forget about that seductive dance! That is out of the question. But I think I could hunker. All I

16

have to do is squat down, close my eyes halfway, and look mean. I don't even have to breathe.

I know that when Rob trips over me, he'll say something like, "What are you doing here? Can't you see we're trying to play a game?" That's when I'll look up at him and flutter my eyelashes, and he'll go "Wow!" and sink down in the dirt next to me and take me in his arms.

Annie says I am definitely very weird, but she doesn't care how I do it as long as I do it. She says if I don't do it, I am a hopeless case, and she will not discuss this boy or any other boy with me ever again. I keep wondering what the odds are that I will be transformed from an ordinary, shy person into a femme fatale in one week.

Guts

I would have done it. I really believe I would have done it. Everything was going fine. I watched Rob play for four days, and I swear I noticed him glancing over at me. Every time I caught his eye, he looked away so fast that I got the idea that maybe he was embarrassed, too. That gave me courage.

Every evening after supper, I met Annie at the playground on the corner between her apartment and mine. It's summer vacation, and every summer since we started junior high, Annie and I have been meeting at the playground in the evening. Before that, I used to go to Annie's. She lives in the same building as Grandma. That's how I met her. I went to Grandma's after school because my parents didn't want me to be home alone while they were at work. For a long time Annie watched me from the landing above Grandma's apartment. She never said anything, but I knew she was up there watching. Then one day, while I was waiting for Grandma to let me in, Annie came up behind me and asked, "How come you always here? Ain't you got a mama?"

"Of course I've got a mommy," I said. "But I like my grandma, too."

"My grandmama lives with me," Annie told me.

I didn't know what to say to that. Luckily, Grandma opened the door, and Annie disappeared.

But the next day she was waiting for me outside on the stoop. "Tell your grandmama you'll be playing at my house today," she said. And that was that.

Annie has three brothers and four sisters and more aunts and cousins than I can keep track of. There's always shouting and laughing and singing at Annie's. Everyone is speaking Spanish, so I don't understand what they're saying. Sometimes Annie even forgets and starts speaking Spanish to me, but I don't mind. My mom's a nurse and she has to get up at five-thirty to go to work, so she goes to bed really early. Then Dad and I have to be quiet, so we won't disturb her. At Annie's it never occurs to anyone to be quiet. I like it.

But the summer before we started junior high Annie decided that we had to be more grown-up and independent if we were going to survive in junior high school. So, we started meeting at the playground. Mom and Dad let me go because the playground is lit up really bright at night, and half the neighborhood is there. In the daytime it's all mothers and little children.

But at night everybody is out trying to keep cool. Annie and I sit on the swings and talk. The week I was carrying out the strategy, I had to give Annie a progress report every day. On the seventh day, Annie said, "Tomorrow's the big day, Marty." I nodded and started pumping until I was swinging high and fast. I threw my head back and laughed out loud. The motion of the swing made a breeze on my face and arms and toes. I felt like I was going somewhere.

When I stopped pumping and let the swing slow down, I saw Annie sitting still on her swing, twisting her thick black hair around her fingers, watching me.

"What?" I said.

"You've got magic. Can you feel it?"

The next day I woke up early. I didn't want to get to the park too soon, and Annie was working at McDonald's, so I skated over to my grandmother's apartment. I drove her crazy, hanging around, asking questions about Baldy. She said he was a good man and very kind to her. Whatever that means.

While Grandma made me lunch, I read my horoscope in the newspaper. "A good day to start new projects," it said.

"That's a wonderful idea," said Grandma. "Then you'd get out of my hair."

"What kind of new projects do you think I should start?"

"Maybe stamp collecting." Grandma was teasing me, but I didn't care. I knew what that horoscope meant.

I timed it well. When I got to the park, the game was

almost over. Rob looked over at me, and I waved. I'm not positive, but I think he smiled. My plan was to catch him out there on the field before he got back to his friends. I'd have to move fast, so I waited, wound up, like a jack-in-the-box ready to pop.

Then something went wrong. I saw him out of the corner of my eye. The guy Rob was with that day on the path. He was waiting for Rob, too. I could feel him staring at me. I didn't even have to look. I skated away before the game ended, still wound up tight.

"He ruined it," I told Annie. "I can't do it with him there."

"Keep going back," Annie said. "There's got to be a day when he don't show up."

"I can't." I kicked at the dirt under the swings. I didn't need Annie to tell me the magic was gone.

Annie doesn't know when to give up. She says I ought to find out where this boy lives and hang around outside his house. She's nuts.

The truth is, I stopped going to the park, and started riding the subway instead. Annie is disgusted with me.

"I can't believe you, Marty," she said to me. "What you want to ride around on the dark, dirty, smelly subway for when you could be outside enjoying the sunshine?" During the summer Annie spends every day wishing she was sunbathing on the roof of her building, instead of working at McDonald's. "At the end of the summer you gonna be fat and flabby and pasty white and nobody's gonna look at you."

"Fat and flabby?" I poked my stomach.

"All right—skin and bones and pasty white. You know what I mean, girl. If you want that boy to look at you, you got to give him something to look *at.*"

"Annie," I said with great superiority, "there's more to life than Prospect Park."

Dad doesn't mind that I'm riding the subway. When I told him about it, he laughed and said it was a phase I was going through.

"You're searching for yourself, Martini." Dad is kind of literal-minded.

"It's not a phase, Harry," said Mom. "She's bored. That's her problem." She turned to me. "I thought you told me the Morrisons wanted you to sit for them this summer." When I didn't answer, Mom added, "It's dangerous to ride the subway, Marty. You never know where you'll end up."

That's the whole point. But my mother has no sense of adventure. If you think like her, you'd never go anywhere. Last year we read an essay in English class that said some people are so afraid of life they end up staying in bed and eating milk toast, and miss out on it all in the end. I don't know what milk toast is, and I have a strict policy of never asking stupid questions in English class, but you definitely get the idea. Even if you don't know what milk toast is.

I told my mom about the milk toast. She was not impressed. She said, "Marty, go call the Morrisons and stop talking nonsense."

I didn't call the Morrisons. I went to meet Annie at

the playground. I sat on one of the swings and pulled out a stack of cards I'd torn off ads in the subway.

Power up your future!

Create your future!

Train to be a bank teller in only three weeks! High school not required.

All those signs have little cards attached that say "Take One." So I do. While I waited for Annie, I sorted through them, trying to decide whether to be a computer programmer or a dog groomer.

"Watcha doing?" Annie asked when she arrived.

"Planning my future."

"Don't waste your time. Somebody's going to drop the Big One before we get to have a future."

I ignored her and kept looking through my cards. I decided to send them all in. Then when the brochures arrived, I'd keep them under my bed, because you never know what you'll be interested in in years to come.

"Let me see," Annie said finally.

I passed her a few of the cards.

" 'Power up your future!' What a joke!"

"Yeah? Well, at least I won't end up working at McDonald's for the next forty years."

"Don't make me laugh, Marty. 'Power up your future'? You ain't even got the guts to talk to that boy. Instead, you ride around on the subway all day like a bum."

"Look who's talking about guts. Why don't you have a boyfriend if you've got so many guts?"

"At least I got a job. You don't do nothing."

"I've got to go."

23

HORACE W. STURGIS LIBRARY
KENNESAW STATE COLLEGE

"Where you going? You got an important appointment? Going to create your future?"

I left the playground and walked over to my grandmother's apartment. She wasn't home. Ever since she started hanging around with Baldy, she's never home. Baldy likes to bowl, so Grandma's taken up bowling. I think they even joined a league.

I didn't feel like going home, so I got on the subway again. Mom absolutely forbade me to ride the subway at night. She said if it was a phase I was going through, it would have to be a daytime phase because it was too dangerous to be a nighttime phase. She was right. It was creepy riding the subway at night. So, I grabbed a card that said *Free Legal Advice* in case someone mugged me, got off at the next stop, and walked home on the busiest street.

Balance

I didn't enjoy riding the subway the next day. It was Annie's fault. Every time I read one of those ads for Ward's Secretarial School, I could hear Annie's voice sneering "Power up your future!" like a dare.

I felt like seeing Grandma. I wanted to ask her if she thought riding the subway qualified as a "new project." The subway goes directly to nine parks, four cemeteries, and a zoo. Not to mention Far Rockaway. You could spend years exploring all the places the subway goes.

I got off at Canal Street and took the D train back toward Brooklyn. I never went to Grandma's, though. Instead, I got off at Seventh Avenue and walked through Grand Army Plaza. I sat on the steps of the museum and put on my skates. Then I skated through the park.

The baseball game was still going on. Rob didn't notice me at first, but when he went up to bat, he glanced in my direction. He was probably looking for his friend. I didn't wave this time. He stared straight at me. Then he pushed the hair out of his eyes, turned away, and swung the bat with all his strength three times.

Rob hit the ball low and hard. One of the outfielders scooped it up and threw it to the second baseman. Rob started toward second base but he had to run back to first. The next guy struck out. Then there were two more singles, which put Rob on third base. The pop fly that came next was the third out, so Rob never made it home.

Rob's friend still wasn't there as they went into the last half of the ninth inning. Rob plays outfield, which was perfect. As long as the guy didn't show up, I would have plenty of time to catch Rob before he got back to the rest of the team. I reached in my pocket and felt the little cards from the subway. *Power up your future!* I whispered inside my head.

Nothing much happened in the outfield that inning. One guy walked, one struck out, and two more were tagged before they reached first base. Rob must have been bored. He looked over at me seven times. I guess there was nothing else to do.

The game ended, and I glanced around quickly. Maybe Annie was right—there had to be a day when he didn't show up. I set off across the field, forgetting that I still had my skates on till I stumbled on the grass and rough ground. I kept going. There wasn't time to take them off.

I knew I must look ridiculous skating across a softball field. *Grow up, Marty. Nobody skates anymore.* That's what Annie always tells me. *Especially on softball fields,* I added, as I almost tripped. Catching my balance, I caught sight of someone behind me. He was there, watching. I hesitated, not sure what to do. But it was too late. Rob was coming toward me. There was no way out.

I skated right up to him and almost fell into his arms when I lost my balance again. He stepped backward.

"I've been watching you play," I said.

"Oh, yeah?"

We stared at each other. I knew it was the perfect moment for the seductive dance, or at least an eyelash flutter. I willed my eyelashes to flutter. *Come on, eyelashes,* I pleaded. *It's not that big an effort. I know you can do it.* I even tried bribery—long naps, shorter hours. Nothing worked. My stupid eyes stayed wide open, staring at him, and he stared right back.

Something had to happen. I think it's only in science fiction that people get stuck, frozen in time. In real life something has to happen. We both spoke at the same moment. I said, "Well, do you think . . . ?"

He said, "How about . . . ?"

Then we both laughed.

"Come on," he said, and started to walk. I turned around. His friend was gone. This time when I stumbled, Rob grabbed my arm and laughed. "Not the best skating rink," he said. We sat on a bench, and I took off my skates. We walked through the whole park. When I got tired, he carried my skates. I carried his mitt. Then he slipped his hand into mine and left it there.

When we went out on the street because it was getting to be dinnertime, we let go of each other's hands and went down the street in opposite directions. I didn't look back at him over my shoulder. But all the way home I kept looking down at my empty hand, and I had to shift my balance to make up for where I had lost that other part of me.

Spaces

Annie is taking all the credit. She says if it wasn't for her, I would have probably spent the rest of my life riding the subway. She says sometimes you have to be tough with the people you love, especially when you know what's good for them, and they're acting like fools.

I don't say anything. But secretly I am just a little bit proud of myself for being so brave. Besides, I'm the one who has a boyfriend, not Annie.

You'd never know it, though. When I meet Annie at the playground, I have to tell her every single detail of what Rob and I did that afternoon. There isn't all that much to tell. Mostly we walk through the park and hold hands. Rob doesn't even like to talk much. Annie says he's probably shy, and I should make my move. She says if I don't, I will have no one to blame but myself if I end up a lonely old-maid virgin who talks to her cats. Annie has a very colorful imagination.

But maybe I don't want to "make a move." Maybe I like holding hands in the park.

I've never met anybody like Rob. I couldn't have been more wrong about him. One day I told him about seeing him in the office and imagining all the terrible things he had done. Rob laughed.

"Don't remind me. That was the worst day of my life."

"Why? What happened?"

"I got caught cheating."

"Cheating?" He'd already told me he made the honor roll every term last year, and I know he studies about five hours a night when school is on.

"I let a friend of mine copy a paper I wrote," Rob said. "I know I shouldn't have, but I really wanted to help Brent."

"Who's Brent?"

"He's my best friend."

Of course, it had to be the guy who used to wait for Rob after the games. The unshaved guy with the big boots. He looked like someone who would cheat.

"I think I saw you with him once, walking through the park. He turned around and whistled at me."

Rob laughed. "Yeah. That's Brent."

"He goes to our school? I never saw him before."

"He doesn't show up much. He's not too crazy about school."

"I hate to say this, but your friend looked like a sort of unsavory character."

"Unsavory?"

"Yeah. Unsavory."

"Where do you get these words from, Marty?"

"*I* go to school."

Rob shot me a look. I don't know what got into me. I didn't mean to be nasty, but I couldn't help it. It really bothered me that there was someone that Rob cared about so much that he would cheat for him.

Rob was pressing two fingers against his forehead, as if he were either deep in thought or else he had a terrible headache.

"Look, Marty," he said, without taking his fingers away from his forehead, "I know what I did was wrong. But I've known Brent ever since I was a baby. He's a year older than I am, and I used to follow him around, trying to do everything he did. I idolized him. I wanted to be just like him."

"Do you still?" Now that I knew him, I couldn't imagine Rob idolizing somebody like that.

Rob shrugged. "Not exactly. He's not the way he seems, though." Rob sounded defensive. "I mean, he has a really hard time, but he's . . . I don't know. I can't explain it."

I felt Rob pulling away from me. I didn't want to leave it like that.

"What's he like?" I asked.

"He's sensitive," Rob said. "He notices things. And he cares a lot. But he won't let anyone see that. Unless you know him really well, or . . ."

"Or what?"

"Or see his drawings. He's an amazing artist. But he draws comics mostly, so nobody takes his drawing seriously. His parents think he's wasting his time. All they care about is grades. They don't even want to see what he draws."

"So, is that why you let him copy your paper—so he wouldn't get in trouble with his parents?"

"Just so he wouldn't flunk English. He says he doesn't care about finishing high school. He says he'll never get into art school anyway, and it doesn't matter. But I want him at least to have a chance."

"I think I understand," I said.

Rob looked over at me. "Yeah. Well, it backfired anyway. We both got caught."

"So, what happened?"

"My dad had to come down for a meeting with the principal. They take cheating very seriously."

"I bet he was thrilled about that."

"I've never seen him so mad. He lost it completely. He told Mr. Vincent that he expected the school to punish me severely, and he would personally guarantee that it would never happen again. Then he started yelling at me right there in the office. Mr. Vincent said, 'Maybe we should let Rob explain what happened.' But my father said there was nothing to explain. My behavior was inexcusable. When he left, Mr. Vincent sat behind his desk for a minute, thinking. Then he said, "Why don't you go back to class, Robert?"

"What did your dad say when he got home?"

"He came back late that night. I was in my room. I heard my mother ask where he'd been, but Dad didn't answer her. He came straight into my room without knocking and said, 'Robert, I've been at church praying for your immortal soul. I think you had better do the same.' And he walked out."

"Did you?"

"What?"

"Pray."

"Yeah. I prayed. I prayed that Dad would forgive me. I knew God would understand about Brent."

"You believe in God?"

Rob nodded. "Don't you?"

"I don't know."

I couldn't remember ever thinking about it very much. My parents never say much about religion one way or the other. My grandmother does, but you can't take it too seriously. She calls Jesus "The Rabbi," and whenever she has a problem, she has a little chat with "The Rabbi." She says it makes her feel better. Once I told her that she shouldn't call Jesus "The Rabbi" because Jewish people might think she was making fun of them and get offended. Grandma just patted me on the arm and said, "Don't be silly, Marty. Jesus was a Jew. We're all one big family." Ever since then, I've had the feeling that Grandma believes in that one big family more than she believes in Jesus.

So, God has never been a big part of my life.

"It's not like I think God is an old man with a white

beard," Rob said. "It's not something you can touch. God is the only way I can make sense out of the world. It's the reason for everything."

I'd never felt like that. About anything. I tried to understand. And the more I tried, the more alone I felt. I was jealous, like the day I followed those black guys in the park and saw how they all moved together, connected. *Is that what Rob feels,* I wondered. *Is he connected to God like that?*

Rob stood up again and started to walk. I watched him for a minute till he turned around and said, "Aren't you coming?"

We left the Japanese garden and walked around behind it. There was an old toolshed half-hidden behind overgrown bushes. I'd never noticed it before. Rob hoisted himself up on the roof and reached over to help me up. The metal roof was rusting away in places, and one of the holes was big enough for a person to get through. Rob dropped his mitt and my skates through the hole. Then he squeezed through it himself. I followed him.

Inside there were old garden tools and rags. The sun was coming through spaces between the boards. Rob stood near the wall, almost touching it, but not quite. A tiny space between him and the wall.

I could feel his body near me, but I felt the space between us, too. A space all around him. *Is God in that space?*

I knew Rob wanted to share something with me. But

I couldn't touch him. There was that space all around him with God in it, and I couldn't reach through.

Rob turned to face me. "I come here to be alone," he said.

Love Letters and Tarantulas

I see Rob only in the afternoon. I have to go home for supper because that's the one time my family is all together. Even when I was little and practically lived at Annie's, I always had to be home at six o'clock. The first time I played at Annie's, Annie's mom came in and asked if I wanted to stay for supper. "Supper?!" I shrieked, and ran out without saying good-bye. Annie's mother was insulted, but I came back later and ate three helpings of caramel pudding, so she forgave me.

In the summer, when it stays light later and I don't have any homework, my parents don't mind if I go out again after we eat. Mom goes to bed early anyway, and Dad sits in the living room and reads the paper. I used to go over to Annie's or Grandma's. Of course, now that we're so grown up, Annie and I meet at the playground instead.

One day I asked Rob if he wanted to meet me after supper, but he said he'd better not. Rob's family is very close. They spend most of their free time together. And besides, his parents are strict. They worry about bad influences and don't allow Rob to go out in the evening unless he's going to some kind of organized activity at school or at the church. Rob's parents think he's too young to have a girlfriend.

"Still, I don't see why he has to be home with his family every night," I complained to Annie. "Or at least he could invite me over there."

I kind of liked the idea of being part of Rob's family, especially since I hardly ever go over to Annie's anymore. Rob has an old-fashioned mother—the kind who stays home and bakes cookies. I don't think I know anybody whose mother bakes cookies. Even my grandmother refuses to bake cookies. I once told her that grandmothers were supposed to do things like bake cookies, and that she was probably being negligent. Grandma burst out laughing. "Why bake," she shouted, "when they've got all those perfectly good store-bought cookies?!"

"How would you get there?" Annie asked. She'd been quiet so long, pumping on her swing, that I'd almost forgotten about her and Rob and was dreaming about homemade chocolate-chip cookies instead.

"Rob could come get me." Rob lived on the far side

of the park, and I knew my parents would never let me go over there alone at night.

"Yeah. And how would you get home?"

"Oh, I don't know!" I was getting exasperated. "That's not the point. If he really wanted me to come over, we could figure it out."

"Personally, I'm kind of fond of this old playground," Annie muttered.

Rob didn't interfere with anything. I could still visit Grandma in the morning, hang out with Annie in the evening, and be home faithfully for supper every day. In fact, no one even had to know he existed unless I told them. The only people I told were Annie and Grandma. When I told Grandma, she stopped in the middle of washing the floor and looked me up and down.

"Well, well," she said.

"Well, well?"

Grandma nodded.

"Are you surprised?" I asked her.

"No. Not really. I just forget sometimes that you're all grown up." She put down the mop and sat in the living room. "Tell me about him."

I told her about baseball and his blond hair falling in his eyes and holding hands in the park. I even told her about God and Rob's family and feeling left out.

"I don't know about you, Marty."

"What do you mean?"

"Some girls would be happy. You've got a fellow that

you see every afternoon in the park. You've got a best friend you see every evening. You've even got a grandmother who puts up with your nonsense. Heaven knows why." She winked at me.

She was right. I didn't realize how good I had it until Annie started working nights. It was only for a week, while someone went on vacation. But I think you can probably die of boredom in a week. Or at least it could cause permanent psychological damage.

The first night I tried staying home and watching TV, but it was all reruns, and they were bad enough the first time. The second night I went over to the playground. Annie's sister Tonia was there with her friends. She asked me if I wanted to play hopscotch. I still like hopscotch, but I knew Annie would kill me if she found out I was playing hopscotch with her little sister, so I told Tonia I had to go see my grandmother. It was a lie, but once I said it, I had to go. I knew she wouldn't be there. She's out with Baldy almost every night these days. I guess that's one good thing about having a boyfriend who is already bald. You don't have to worry about whether his parents will let him go out with you at night.

After I rang Grandma's bell about ten times, I started walking. I didn't want to ride the subway because I thought it would be awfully sad to get murdered just when I'd found someone to hold hands with in the park. When you walk, most of the strangest people are passed out in doorways, which is depressing but not so dangerous.

I stayed on the main streets where there are stores.

The fruit stands stay open late, and I looked everything over very carefully, squeezed the peaches and plums and nectarines to make sure they were just the right amount of ripe, and then I went and bought an ice-cream cone. While I was eating my ice cream, I looked in the windows of the other stores and tried to figure out what kind of person decides to open a discount variety store. I wanted to know if the people who own those stores ever used to ride the subway and look at the signs that say "Power Up Your Future," and finally decided that instead of learning shorthand, they'd rather sell hats.

I walked every night that week. It was something to do. Each night I went a little farther, hoping to see something interesting. By the end of the week, I was pretty far from home. I knew I should turn back, but I didn't want to. I came to a school. An elementary school. Not the one I went to, but they all look alike. Brick with construction-paper bunnies still pasted to the windows, left over from last spring. I wanted to go inside. I wanted to rummage through the teachers' desks and find out if the stories we used to make up were true. Did Miss Fernandez hide love letters tied with a pink ribbon in her desk? And did Mrs. Anderson actually have a tarantula in a box, and maybe even a rattlesnake that she used to torture the bad kids who had to stay after school? Or would all those drawers be empty with nothing in them but a few pieces of old white chalk rolling around?

I tried every door of that school on the chance that one of them had been left open. I would have tried the windows, too. Annie always says that persistence pays off. Every time I'm ready to give up because not one single store has Oreo-cookie ice cream and I'm willing to settle for fudge swirl, Annie says, "Let's try one more place." She takes me about twenty blocks on the hottest day of the year, and I hate her the whole way, but then we find a place that has it, and as I crunch down on a piece of Oreo, Annie smiles, gloating. She doesn't even have to say, "Sure beats fudge ripple, don't it?" because even though I'm mad, I know that it does.

I thought Annie would be proud of me if I tried all the windows. Probably the very last window would be unlocked, and I'd slide it open and sneak in and look through fifty-seven empty teachers' desks, each with five drawers, and find nothing but old erasers and hardened chewing gum. Then, in the last drawer of the last desk, I'd find a hastily scrawled note:

Darling Miranda,
> *Your cherry lips drive me wild. Meet me in the library storeroom at 2 P.M.*

> > > *Yours forever,*
> > > *William*

I would run over to McDonald's and tell Annie to develop a sudden illness. Then we'd go in the restroom and lock the door and I would whisper, "Look, Annie! It's true—teachers do have passionate affairs! I've got proof." Annie's eyes would light up, and we'd read the note over at least fifteen times. I'd call Mom and tell her

I was sleeping over at Annie's. Then we'd stay up all night making up stories about Miranda and William.

That's what would have happened. Except when I got to the last door and shoved against it, I heard someone behind me say, "Hey, Marty, you like school so much you just can't bear to stay away?"

I envy those women in the olden days who always used to faint. Or swoon, I think they called it then. "Ah, me," they'd sigh, and swoon. Unfortunately, swooning has gone out of style. Instead, I had to turn around and face Rob's friend.

The one from the park.

I hadn't seen him since the first day I talked to Rob. He stopped meeting Rob at the end of the games. I guess it's because of me.

"Watcha doing?" he asked.

"Nothing much."

"You bored?"

"No! I just—"

"Sure, you are. It's nothing to be ashamed of. I've been friends with Rob ever since we were little babies. I know the scene. Rob's a family man. He never goes out. The guy doesn't know what it means to party. He's a good kid. But if you're hanging around with Rob, you got to be bored at night. I know." He winked.

I didn't say anything. I was hoping he would go away.

"Come on," he said. "I'll introduce you to my other friends. That'll make your life more exciting. These guys are crazy!"

"I ought to get home."

"What're you scared of? They're not dangerous or anything."

"I'm not scared."

"So, come on."

He walked away and didn't even look back to see if I was coming. I could have left then and gone home, but instead I followed him. He cut through an empty lot near the school, pushed aside some boards from the window of an abandoned building, and waited till I caught up.

"My name's Brent," he said.

"I know."

"All right, Miss Know-It-All. After you."

I climbed through the window. Brent's friends were drinking beer and laughing. They had a boom box hooked up to a car battery and were playing heavy metal, but not so loud you could hear it outside.

Brent said, "Hey, guys, this is Marty." And that was it. He didn't say I was Rob's girlfriend or even explain how he knew me. He told them my name, and then he ignored me. Everybody ignored me. The boys kept drinking, and the girls smoked cigarettes and hung on the boys. Brent didn't have a girl hanging on him, and I couldn't figure out why. He's not exactly good-looking, but there's something about him. . . . Since I have a boyfriend, I knew I shouldn't be thinking about things like that, but I had to have something to think about while I was standing there looking stupid.

I didn't know how to get out of there. I thought about asking Brent if there was a bathroom and going and hiding in it for about twenty minutes, but that seemed even dumber than standing around. Besides, the water's turned off in those old buildings, so I didn't even want to think about what the bathrooms would be like. When Brent offered me a beer, I took it, even though I hate beer. I needed something to do with my hands and my mouth. My mind was busy, saying over and over, *Well, I guess I'd better be going now.* That seemed simple enough, but the longer I didn't say anything, the harder it got. After all that silence, I knew everyone would stare at me for sure.

Finally Brent said, "Come on, Marty, I'll take you home."

"Okay."

"Hey, Jimmy, let me take your bike," Brent said.

"All right, son, but be careful now, and don't come home too late." The boy named Jimmy tossed Brent his keys. Brent leaped into the air, yelping with pleasure.

"Oh, mama! I got the keys to the car! I'm gonna cruise tonight!"

He was drunk. I figured I probably shouldn't ride with him. I didn't even know if he had a license. But it was getting really late, and I had to get home.

Brent got on the motorcycle first, and I climbed on behind him. I didn't know what to do with my hands.

"Hold on," he said. I put my hands on his waist. His body was warm under his T-shirt. He started the bike and suddenly there was noise and wind. We rode back past the school and all the fruit stands so fast it made my life before seem as if it had been in slow motion. I'd never been on a motorcycle before. It was better than swinging high and fast. Much better.

I didn't want my parents to see me on a motorcycle with a boy, so I asked Brent to let me off at the playground, and I walked home.

"Come back tomorrow," Brent said as he roared away.

Come back tomorrow? He must be crazy.

Best Friends

I didn't tell Rob about running into Brent. I know he would feel bad if he knew that I was walking around the streets alone at night trying to break into elementary schools. He'd feel torn between me and his family.

I didn't tell Annie about Brent, either. I wanted to, but we were going to the beach with Rob the next day, so I didn't have a chance to talk to her alone. It was Annie's last day of working nights. I was ecstatic, but Annie was in a deep depression. The only thing that cheered her up a little was that she was finally going to meet Rob.

"Sure," I said. I didn't really think Rob would come. He didn't have a game that day, just practice. Still, I know he likes to play every day. But when I asked him about the beach, he never even mentioned baseball.

That's how I knew he must be feeling guilty.

Annie liked Rob right away. I thought it was going to be awkward because they have nothing in common except for me. I couldn't imagine what we would talk about. But as soon as we got on the subway, Annie and Rob started talking about working conditions at McDonald's, and by the time we got to the beach, they were discussing independence for Puerto Rico. I was beginning to feel a little left out, but Rob held my hand the whole time, and when we got off the subway and Annie stopped to get a Coke, Rob took my hand and laid it on his cheek. Then he looked into my eyes. It was much better than talking.

Rob and I were still gazing at each other when Annie came back, swinging her beach bag over her head like a cowboy and calling out in a loud voice, "Okay, love-birds. Let's go soak up some rays!"

Usually Annie is very serious about sunbathing. As soon as we get to the beach, she lays out her towel, rubs herself with suntan oil, and cannot be disturbed for at least two hours. At first I didn't understand it because Annie's skin is already the most beautiful golden brown, even if she never lies out in the sun. Then I figured out that it's not the color that she cares about. Annie loves the feel of the hot sun all over her body. She says it's in her genes—she wasn't meant to live in a place where it's cold and snowing half the year, so in the summer she has to soak up all the sun she can and store it up for winter, like a squirrel does with nuts.

But that day Annie didn't even lie down. She sat on

the edge of her towel, dug her toes into the sand, and talked to Rob. When they got tired of serious topics, Annie told funny stories about her family. Rob loved it. I never saw him laugh so hard. And even though I had heard all the stories several times before, I laughed, too.

When Annie finally got around to some serious sunbathing, Rob and I took a walk along the boardwalk.

"Annie's a character," Rob said. Then he added, "I like her."

"I like her, too," I said.

"Gee, I hope so," Rob said. "She is your best friend."

Then we both burst out laughing.

I knew Annie would be undisturbable for at least a couple of hours, so Rob and I took our time. We walked a long way, holding hands. Then we sat on a bench on the boardwalk and watched the people. A man with tattoos all over his chest was feeding peanut butter and jelly sandwiches to two tiny children. A woman was playing tag with her daughter, both their heads beaded with matching braids and cornrows. And an old man was playing the blues on a saxophone. I was glad to see there were even a few people on roller skates. I wanted Rob to know that I'm not the only weirdo in the city who still skates.

We walked back slowly with our arms around each other. I didn't notice till we got up close that Annie was sitting up again, watching us approach.

On the way home Annie was much quieter, sleepy and contented from the sun. Rob put his arm around me and I leaned my head against his shoulder and fell asleep. Annie was singing softly to herself in Spanish.

Annie and I left Rob on the subway and walked home. I was waiting for Annie to say something about what she thought of Rob, but she was absolutely silent until we got to the entrance to my building. Then she turned to me with the strangest expression on her face. It was a look of amazement, as if she'd never really noticed what I looked like before. "He adores you," she said. Then she smiled and walked away.

I watched her walk down the street until she turned the corner at the playground. I hugged myself tightly and said softly, "Yeah, he does."

That night I stayed home. I was much too tired to walk around the streets and much too happy to be bored.

Two days later Brent showed up at the park. When I got to the baseball field, there he was, leaning against the fence.

"Hi," I said.

"How come you didn't come back?" he asked.

"Why should I?"

He turned around and leaned his back against the fence so he could look at me.

"Because I want to talk to you."

"Talk to me? You didn't say a word to me the whole time. I felt like a jerk."

"I'm sorry." He sounded more angry than sorry. But at me? Or at himself? I couldn't tell. He lit a cigarette.

The game ended, and I heard the guys behind us joking about the great plays they'd almost made. Brent took a drag on his cigarette, taking his time.

"So, how about it? Will you come back?"

"Hey, Brent!" Rob shouted. Brent turned to him, grinning.

"No," I whispered. But I doubt if he heard me.

Rob and I started walking, and Brent came along. I could tell Rob was happy to see him. He didn't even mind when Brent put his arm around me and said, "Where have you been all my life, sweetheart?"

Rob said, "Hey, man, watch where you put those hands. You know what I mean?"

But I could tell he wasn't really mad.

Brent pushed Rob's baseball hat down over his eyes and said, "Some guys have all the luck."

Rob chased him, and they wrestled on the grass till they got tired. Then Rob got up, brushed off his hat, and put it on backward. He took my hand, and we walked Brent as far as the entrance to the park.

While we were walking, Brent told us about getting chased by the police the night before. He said that he and his friends were hanging out on Seventh Avenue. They weren't even drunk because they couldn't find anyone to buy for them. But the cops came along and told them to move.

"You guys should've been there," Brent told us. "Jimmy was awesome. He said, 'This is a public street, ain't it? And we are the public. So, why don't you boys get lost? Ain't you got no real criminals in this town?

You guys bored or somethin'?' The boys in blue started getting mean. They've got no manners, you know. They started pushing Jimmy around, shoving him, saying, 'Watch your mouth, punk.' Jimmy pushed back, and pretty soon we were all fighting."

"Did they take you in?" Rob asked.

"You got it, buddy-boy."

"They did?!" I had the feeling my mouth was hanging open. I felt like a baby.

"Yeah." Brent smiled at me. "It's no big deal, sweetheart. The police pick me up all the time."

"Did your dad come down and get you?" Obviously Rob had heard all this before.

"He sure did. He loves that. Getting a call in the night—'Mr. Conrad? This is Officer Franklin. Your son has been picked up for disorderly conduct.' Poor guy. Must be tough on an upstanding citizen. I don't even bother to call him anymore. I can't deal with him. I'd rather spend the night in jail, but the police don't want me around, either, so they—"

"What's going to happen, Brent?" Rob interrupted.

"I don't know, man." We'd come to the gate of the park. Brent slipped through it and disappeared down the street without saying good-bye.

Rob was quiet for a long time. He was thinking about something. We were walking side by side, but I wasn't quite sure he remembered I was there.

"Rob?" I said finally.

"What?"

"Talk to me."

"Sorry," he said. "I was thinking about Brent. I wish I could figure out how to help him."

"You do help him. He knows you care about him. That helps."

"But he hardly ever comes around anymore. I never know if he's okay. Or if he's in trouble or in jail. Or even alive."

He didn't say it was my fault, but I felt it.

"Maybe it would be better if I didn't meet you here every day."

Rob didn't answer me. He put his arm around me and squeezed my shoulder. Then he said, "I worry too much. Let's talk about something else." But he didn't answer me.

Bruised

I never had to decide whether to stop meeting Rob every day because Brent started showing up at the park all the time. Whenever I got there, Brent was there, waiting. Of course, Rob thought Brent was waiting for him, and it made him really happy. He kept trying to get Brent to join the game, but Brent always refused. I had a feeling I knew why.

One day he said to me, "So, is this the only way I'm ever going to get to see you?"

"I guess so," I said.

"Why won't you come back?"

"I'm busy," I answered. "I got a job baby-sitting."

"How convenient," he said.

It's sort of true, though. I did call the Morrisons. Mrs. Morrison works in the mornings, while her son goes to day camp. She wanted somebody to meet him at the bus at noon and give him lunch. That way she wouldn't have to worry if she was running late. She's always home by one o'clock. Two at the absolute latest. I don't even have to worry about the baby since she's in day care, and Mrs. Morrison picks her up on her way home. So, I told her I'd do it. It's only an hour or two a day, and I can still meet Rob every afternoon. I also told her I was available in the evening. She calls me about twice a week.

Mom is thrilled that I have something "constructive" to do now. She was worried about me. Riding the subway was bad enough, but when the brochures started arriving from Taylor's Technical School, she had a fit. "You're going to finish high school, Marty. And then you are going to college. And that's all there is to it." I ignored her, and hid the brochures under my bed. But when I told her I was going to baby-sit for the Morrisons, she smiled as though she had won the lottery. I don't know what Mom thinks is so great about baby-sitting. Personally I would rather groom poodles than be a baby-sitter. For one thing, if I keep baby-sitting, I will probably die of malnutrition before I even reach adulthood. The Morrisons never cook. The baby doesn't eat real food yet, and her brother eats only bologna sandwiches, so Mrs. Morrison leaves out a frozen dinner for me. I have to flush it down the toilet. I hate to do it because I think it's a crime to throw away food when people are starving. Dad told me not to worry about it because the government throws away millions of tons of food every year or every day or something, so my little frozen dinner hardly matters. Besides, he says, who knows if those things are even food? Still, it bothers me.

I don't think it's fair for the Morrisons to confront me with a moral dilemma every time I work for them. If people are going to hire a baby-sitter, they ought to be required to take a course in the tastes and needs of teenagers. How could they know anything about it? If their children were teenagers, they wouldn't need a baby-sitter.

Not that the parents of teenagers are much better. Mom doesn't seem to be the least bit concerned about what I eat at the Morrisons'. She doesn't even mind when I have to miss supper. She's happy because the Morrisons live only four blocks away, so I don't have to ride the subway. I walk over while it's still light out, and Mr. Morrison brings me home.

When I get home, I go in the living room and talk to Dad. Dad enjoys hearing about the adventures of a teenaged baby-sitter. He's interested in whether a six-year-old boy will succeed in strangling his baby sister. Usually, before Dad goes to bed, he sums up the evening's events like a soap-opera announcer. "Will the baby come down with the chicken pox? Will her brother strangle her in her sleep? Will the baby-sitter die of malnutrition? Tune in tomorrow for the dramatic continuation of 'As the Baby Spews.'" Then he kisses me and goes to his room.

Dad doesn't take it seriously about my dying of malnutrition, but I think it's dangerous not to eat when you're baby-sitting. It's a terrible responsibility to have a child's life in your hands. If there was a crisis, I might be too weak to respond. I know that's what happened last night.

It was late, and I was watching television, switching from station to station because there was nothing good on. The doorbell rang. I clicked off the TV with the remote control and stopped breathing. I never saw any of those movies where the baby-sitter gets murdered, but I've heard about them. The bell rang again. Sometimes people wander into the front hallway of our building late at night and ring the buzzer. Usually we just ignore it, and they go away. But the Morrisons live on the first floor. The bell rang again. I thought about calling my parents or the police. But what if the police came and it turned out it was a friend of the Morrisons who dropped by to say hello? The bell rang a third time. This time whoever was out there kept ringing and didn't stop. I got worried that the baby would wake up and start screaming, so I went to the door.

"Who is it?"

"Marty? It's me. Brent. Open up."

I didn't know what to do. He sounded drunk.

"Open the door, dammit!" He started pounding on the door. I opened it a crack.

"What are you doing here?"

"I wanna talk to you."

He was drunk for sure. I would've slammed the door, except he looked terrible. The whole left side of his face was bruised and purple, and there was a bloody gash over his eye. I let him in.

"What happened to you?"

"Walked into a lamppost."

"That's not funny."

"No. It's not. They can get awful mean, those lampposts."

"You ought to go to the hospital."

"Nah. I'm all right." He slumped down on the Morrisons' couch.

"How did you know where I was?"

"Followed you. A few days ago. Thought I might want to drop by sometime and keep you company while you're baby-sitting."

"You're crazy."

"Yeah. That's me. Brent Conrad—crazy man."

"Why do you do it?"

"What?"

"You know. Get in trouble all the time."

"Are you a shrink or something? You ought to talk to my folks. They've got all kinds of theories." He swung his arms out wide. "I'm just having me some fun!"

"You've got to get out of here, Brent. The Morrisons could be back anytime."

"Come see me tomorrow night."

I shook my head.

"I'll be waiting for you at that old building."

"Forget it."

"I know you don't baby-sit every night. I've been watching you."

"Why?"

"Don't know. Must be bored."

"Gee, thanks." I opened the door and stood there, waiting for him to leave.

Just then the baby started to cry. Brent was standing near her room. Instead of leaving, he turned and went toward her. I slammed the door and ran after him. He was drunk, and I had no idea what he would do. By the time I got to him, Brent had picked up the baby.

"Give her to me," I said.

Brent looked up. "Shh!" he said to me. He was holding the baby against his chest, rocking her gently. "It's okay," he whispered to her. "Everything's okay."

The baby stopped crying and went back to sleep. Brent didn't turn around, but he knew I was there, watching him.

"My parents always said that one kid was more than enough," Brent said. "I guess they're the kind of people who shouldn't have kids. Still . . ."

"What?"

"I don't know. I always wished I had a brother or a sister."

I was thinking about what Rob had said about following Brent around when they were little.

"You had Rob," I said.

That's right," he responded. "At least I had Rob."

Brent laid the baby back in the crib.

"I should go," he said.

I watched him go to the front door. He turned back to me from the doorway.

"Will you come?" he asked. "Please."

Maybe it was the pain from the gash over his eye that made his face scrunch up like that.

"All right," I said. "I'll come."

When I got home, Dad asked me for his usual report. "Hey, Martini," he said as I came in the door. "Anything exciting happen tonight?"

"No. Nothing much," I said, and went straight to my room.

Calling Names

I pushed the boards aside and stepped through the window. A few people looked up, but they didn't say anything. Brent wasn't waiting for me. I wandered through the building, looking for him, afraid to ask anyone where he was. I felt like an idiot.

"Hey, Marty!"

I was climbing back out the window, and I didn't turn around. Someone ran over and grabbed my foot.

"Where are you going?" It was Jimmy. The guy with the motorcycle. "Brent had to go someplace. He told me to tell you he'd be right back."

"Where'd he go?" I asked.

"I don't know. But he won't be gone long. Come on back inside." He let go of my foot.

"No, thanks," I said.

I was two blocks away when Brent caught up with me. I heard him running down the street, but I didn't stop. He ran past me, then turned and walked backward in front of me. He was out of breath.

"I'm sorry, Marty."

"Why don't you leave me alone?"

"I thought I'd be back before you got there. I had to go out to get beer. It was my turn. Usually I have no problem, but there was a new guy working there, and he didn't believe—"

"Who cares?"

"Come on, Marty. You came all the way down here. You can't go home now without even talking to me."

"I can't? Watch me."

He dropped to his knees right in front of me. I almost tripped over him.

"Please." He clasped his hands in front of him. "Don't do this to me, honey. Don't leave me alone with the seventeen kids. You're breakin' my heart."

I had to laugh. Brent stood up and threw me over his shoulder.

"I knew you'd see it my way," he said as he staggered back the way we'd come. I was still laughing as I beat his back and screamed at him to let me go.

Finally, Brent put me down. "What're you trying to do?" he asked. "Get me arrested? I can manage that without any help. Now, come on."

"I found her," Brent announced to the darkness inside the building. He put one arm around me and grabbed Jimmy's beer with the other hand.

"Thanks, buddy."

"What the—" Jimmy started after him. Brent turned around and blew him a kiss.

"Yeah, I love you, too, man," Jimmy called after us.

The stairs were rotting, but Brent knew exactly where to step. I kept my eyes on his feet, all the way to the third floor, trying not to think about what would happen next. Brent pushed open the door to one of the apartments. It was much lighter up there because not all the windows were boarded up. There were a couple of old, ripped mattresses on the floor near the window. A boy and a girl were lying on one of the mattresses, kissing. I wanted to die of embarrassment, but it didn't seem to bother Brent at all that we had walked in on them. He walked over and stood right above them.

"Hey," he said.

The boy rolled over onto his back and looked up at Brent.

"Hey, Brent. What's happening?"

"What are you doing here, man?"

The boy grinned. "What does it look like?"

Brent didn't smile. "Get out," he said.

"What the hell— You don't own this place."

Brent grabbed him and pulled him to his feet. "Get out!" he said again.

"All right. All right." The boy glanced at me. "Who's this?" he asked. "The Stud's latest conquest?"

The girl stood up, too, and was straightening her clothes. "You skate in the park," she said to me. "I've seen you with that really cute guy. What's his name—Rob?"

I didn't answer.

The boy started to laugh. "Oh, that explains it," he said. "You must have gotten sick of being around someone so holy. No wonder. Rob-the-Saint gives me a pain, too."

I turned to leave. I didn't want to hear any more of this.

"Shut up!" I heard Brent say behind me.

"Lighten up, Brent. The kid's a jerk. What's it to you?"

"He's my best friend," Brent said.

The other guy started to laugh again. I turned around just in time to see Brent grab him by the shoulders and knock him against the wall.

"I thought I told you to get out of here," Brent said.

"You are one sick puppy," the boy said. But he left. The girl followed him.

"I'm sorry, Marty," Brent said.

"I want to go home."

Brent didn't try to stop me. He flopped down on the mattress and picked up Jimmy's beer from where he'd set it on the floor when he first came in. "I don't blame you," he said.

"Thanks for sticking up for Rob," I said.

"That guy who was in here makes me sick. He's always putting other people down." Brent drank some of the beer and held it out to me. I shook my head, but I didn't leave.

Brent turned the can around in his hands. "Marty," he said, as if he were reading the word off the label and he'd never heard it before. "Marty," he repeated thoughtfully. "What's that short for? Martha?"

"Martha?! No! It's not short for anything."

"Marty is on your birth certificate?"

"Yeah. Why not? What's wrong with Marty? It's like Brent. Brent's not short for anything."

"Yes, it is."

"It is?"

"That's right."

"What?"

"Brendan."

"You're lying. It is not."

"Wanna bet?" He pulled out his driver's license. At least he has one. *Brendan Peter Conrad,* it said.

"Why'd you change it?"

"Brendan. What a loser name. It sounds like a banker."

"Brendan Peter Conrad. I think it sounds impressive."

"Impressive as hell."

"All I've got is Marty."

"Marty's all right, I guess."

"I've got nicknames."

"Like what?"

I sat down on the mattress. "Well, my dad calls me Martini. And when I was little he used to call me Martian. He'd come home from work, and I'd run down the stairs to meet him and jump into his arms, and he'd swing me around and say, 'How's my favorite Martian today?' "

"No kidding. You actually jumped in his arms? I thought that only happened on TV." I couldn't tell if he was making fun of me, so I shut up.

"What's the matter?"

"Nothing."

He touched me then, lightly, on the tips of my fingers. "You're lucky," he said. "My dad's not the type of person you could jump on. Dad's idea of affection is a handshake. 'Hello, son, how are you today?' Shake, shake. Can't you picture it? A little five-year-old boy, and Dad's shaking his hand."

Brent laughed, but I didn't. It was sad.

"Come on," he said. "Tell me more about your dad. I want to know."

"For a while he brought me a present every day. Not the usual stuff, no gum or candy, but funny things like a double acorn or one of those red plastic monkeys bartenders put in drinks at bars. Dad likes stuff like that. Every time he goes to the supermarket he has to bring back something new. It's very important to him to know that none of us has ever had it before. So, my mom likes to tease him. 'But Harry,' she says. 'I've had pickled pig's feet lots of times!' We don't actually eat any of it. It's like a collection. Dad even built a special shelf for it in the kitchen."

"That's weird."

"I know. I keep all the stuff he gave me in a shoe box under my bed." I didn't tell him about the brochures for Ward's Secretarial School. That was too personal.

"Marty," Brent said again, rolling it over on his tongue, tasting it. "MARRRTEEE!" he bellowed.

Then he leaned back with his hands behind his head, staring up at the ceiling.

"I like you, Marrrteee," he said, and grinned.

Magnets

For the next three nights I met Brent at the abandoned building. We always went to the same room in the apartment on the third floor. I knew that I shouldn't be meeting Brent, but I couldn't quite figure out why. We never did anything. We just sat on the mattress and talked. Rob wouldn't have any reason to be jealous. In fact, he'd probably be glad that Brent had someone to talk to. He'd probably be relieved to know that Brent was talking to me instead of being out on the street getting into trouble. So, why hadn't I told him?

And then there was Annie. I hadn't seen Annie all week. I hadn't been at the playground to meet her, and I hadn't even called to explain where I was. I didn't do it on purpose. I just didn't think about it. But how do you tell your best friend that you found someone else to talk to every night, and you forgot all about her?

On the fourth night I had to baby-sit for the Morrisons. They had been at the beach all day, and both children were exhausted. The baby was asleep when I got there, and as soon as I fed her brother his bologna sandwich, he fell asleep, too.

It was a perfect opportunity to call Annie and explain where I'd been. The Morrisons wouldn't be home for at least an hour, probably two.

First I rummaged through the cupboards in case the Morrisons had suddenly developed a craving for potato chips or pretzels. Of course, I didn't find anything. I was hungry. I ate some yogurt out of desperation, and the rest of an open jar of puréed banana baby food.

I checked the children. Both were sleeping soundly. Then I went back in the kitchen and picked up the phone. The Morrisons have one of those wall phones in the kitchen. The only other extension is in their bedroom, and I never feel comfortable going in there. So I leaned against the counter and played with the magnets on the refrigerator while I waited for someone to pick up the phone.

Annie's mother answered. When I asked her if Annie was home, she said, "Sure, Marty. I'll get her." Then she yelled *"Anna! Telephone!"* so loudly I probably could have heard it without the phone.

Annie took her time getting to the phone. The magnets were in the shape of the letters of the alphabet. While I waited I spelled my name on the refrigerator.

"Hello?" Annie said.

"Hi, Annie. It's me."

"No kidding. If it ain't Miss Houdini herself. The famous disappearing act. I hope you got a good excuse, girl."

Annie was in a good mood. She didn't even sound that mad. Somehow that made it even harder to tell the truth.

"Well . . ." I began.

"Hold it. I got a better idea. Let's talk about this in person. Meet you at the swings in ten."

"I can't. I'm at the Morrisons'."

"Don't tell me the Morrisons kidnapped you and are holding you hostage so they'll have a live-in baby-sitter."

"Not exactly."

"Look, Marty, you don't gotta be embarrassed. Just tell me that boy Rob finally got his head screwed on right and decided to do right by you. I ain't gonna make you feel guilty. I'm happy for you. 'Course, you could've let me know. But I'll let it slide on account of people in love is known to go slightly out of their minds."

So, that's what she thought. That's why she wasn't mad. She thought Rob finally "made his move," and she was happy for me.

"I wasn't with Rob," I said.

There was a long silence at the other end of the line. I spelled Rob's name under mine on the refrigerator.

"So," she said finally, "where was you?"

"Remember that guy I told you about—Rob's friend?"

"Yeah, sure. The one that almost screwed up my brilliant strategy. What about him?"

"I ran into him one night when you were working.

And he wanted to talk. He's got a lot of problems. I mean, he gets in trouble all the time, and his parents are always coming down on him. So, I—"

"What about Rob?"

"Nothing about Rob. What does this have to do with Rob? All I do is talk to Brent. He's lonely."

"All you do is talk to Rob, too."

"It's different. I love Rob. Brent's just a friend."

"Ain't he Rob's best friend?"

"Yes."

"Oh, wow, Marty. I can't believe this."

"What's the big deal, Annie? I just want to help him. I want to be his friend. What's wrong with that?"

"Does Rob know that you and this guy is 'friends?' "

"No," I said softly.

There was another long silence. I spelled Brent's name on the refrigerator, but I couldn't find another *t,* so I added it on to my name like a crossword puzzle.

"You planning on telling Rob?" Annie asked.

"Of course. Why shouldn't I?"

"I don't know. You tell me. You ain't told him yet."

"It just . . ." There was a tapping at the window. It had to be Brent. I ignored it. "It just didn't seem like that big a deal."

The tapping got louder.

"What's that noise?" Annie asked.

"I'm not sure. I better go check. Can I meet you tomorrow at the playground?"

"Yeah, I guess so."

Brent had pushed the window open a crack and yelled, "Hey, Marty, you deaf? Let me in."

"I'll see you tomorrow," I told Annie, and hung up fast before she could ask any more questions.

"I wish you wouldn't come here," I told Brent when I let him in. "I don't want to get in trouble with the Morrisons."

"You always worry about getting in trouble, Marty? Who were you talking to? Robbie?"

"No. Annie."

"That's right. I forgot. Rob's gotta keep you a secret. Poor sucker. He doesn't know what he's missing."

Brent found the Morrisons' liquor cabinet and started looking through the bottles. He opened a bottle of Jim Beam and raised it to his lips.

"Please don't," I said.

"They won't miss one little slug."

"You're already drunk. I don't like you when you drink."

"Sorry, baby. I can't help it. When you're not around, I don't know what else to do with myself." He took one more slug, then put the bottle back.

"You ought to get help, you know."

He put his arm around me. "You're gonna help me, right?" He leaned close, and I could smell the alcohol on his breath. "Don't you want to help me?"

I pulled away. "Look, Brent . . ."

"Oh-oh. Here it comes. 'Look, Brent. You're a great

guy and everything, but I don't want to see you anymore 'cause you're screwed up, and besides, my boyfriend wouldn't like it.' "

"I didn't say that."

"But you were going to."

"I was going to tell you that Annie's mad at me 'cause I didn't meet her at the playground the past three nights. So I asked her to meet me tomorrow."

"Does that mean you'll be back the day after that?"

I couldn't stay mad at him when he looked at me that way.

I half smiled. "Yeah. I'll be back."

"I better get out of here." He absentmindedly ran his hand over my hair and let it rest on the back of my neck. "I don't want to get you in trouble." He winked at me, then slipped out the door.

I stood in the middle of the living room. I was trembling. *I love Rob*, I said to myself. *I love Rob. I love Rob. I love Rob.* But no matter how many times I repeated it, I couldn't shake off the way I felt when Brent touched the back of my neck.

Annie sat on the swing next to mine.

"I been thinking about this all day," she began, "and I come to the conclusion that there's only one thing you can do."

"What's that?"

"You gotta stop seeing this guy."

"I don't know." She was right, of course. But . . .

"Marty, listen to me. Even if it's true that you just want

to be friends, it ain't fair to him. You're leading him on. That was him making that tapping noise last night, wasn't it?"

"Yes," I admitted.

"Marty, I wasn't born yesterday, and neither was you. A guy don't come banging on the window while you're baby-sitting 'cause he wants to be 'friends.' "

"You're wrong, Annie. You don't know Brent. That's just the way he is, kind of crazy and reckless. He does stuff like that all the time. It doesn't mean anything."

"All right. I thought through all the angles. So, let's say, just for the sake of argument, let's say you're right. You still gotta cut it out. 'Cause it ain't fair to Rob."

I chewed on my lip. "I know I ought to tell Rob. I don't want to hide anything from him. It's just that he feels bad enough that Brent doesn't talk to him anymore, so I thought he'd feel worse if he knew—"

"Marty, you are insulting my intelligence with all this crap. I'm telling you for your own good. What you're doing ain't right. I don't care what you say. You gotta forget about this guy."

I looked at her, begging her to understand. "I can't," I whispered.

Inside Out

Brent used to live at Rob's house the way I lived at Annie's, and Rob's parents treated him like part of the family. But then they decided he was a bad influence on Rob, so he doesn't like to go over there anymore. Instead, he spends most of his time lying on that old mattress in the abandoned building, drawing comics.

"Could I see them sometime?" I asked him once.

"I don't know. Maybe. Sometime."

"Rob says you're really good."

"Yeah. Well, Rob's my friend. He's got to say that."

"What do you think? Are you good?"

Brent shrugged. "It's something to do," he said. Then he asked, "You ever draw or anything?"

"No, not really. Sometimes I write in my journal, but

not very often. I can't sit still long enough to do that kind of stuff. Ever since I was little, I've had trouble sitting still. Mom says I'm always squirming. It drives her crazy. Grandma keeps telling her I'll settle down eventually, but I hope not. I like to keep moving."

Brent laughed. "You part of the jet set, Marty?"

"No." I pulled at the stuffing that was falling out of the mattress. "I can't fly, but . . ." I started to giggle. "I roll."

"Oh, yeah," Brent said. "I've seen you."

"You have?"

"Sure. In the park, remember? You tried to skate across a baseball field. Is that what you call moving?"

I was still giggling, picturing myself traveling all over the world on roller skates. I nodded. Then on an impulse I added, "But that's not all."

"Well, what else?"

"I ride the subway." As soon as I said it, I was sorry.

"Everybody rides the subway. So what?"

"But I don't ride it to get somewhere. I just ride it."

"What for?"

"I don't know." It was hard to explain.

Brent jumped up.

"Let's go," he said.

"Where?"

"Let's go ride the subway."

"I don't know . . ."

"You said you like to keep moving. I feel like going someplace. Let's go to Coney Island."

"Coney Island?"

"Yeah. Coney Island. Go call your parents."

"What for?"

"Because we'll be back late. Make up some excuse."

I called home and told them I was at Annie's because they were having a birthday party for her cousin and not to worry if I got home late. Dad said he'd come pick me up, but I told him there were lots of people there, and I was sure someone could bring me home. I don't usually lie to my parents. I don't always tell them everything, but I don't like to lie out and out. It made me feel funny.

Brent and I rode the subway to Coney Island. On the way we played a game trying to think of all the different ways you could roll, like climbing inside a bowling ball. Brent said the absolute best way to roll was on a roller coaster, and that was the real reason we had to go to Coney Island. I told him that my idea of a good time is bumper cars. I don't believe in anything that turns you upside down, inside out, suspends you in midair, or otherwise defies the laws of physics.

"Screw physics," Brent said, and bought tickets for the Cyclone.

We rode the roller coaster five times. I clutched Brent's arm and screamed.

After the fifth time, Brent said, "I'm starving. Want some pizza?"

I doubted if I would ever eat again, but Brent ate three slices of pepperoni pizza and washed it down with a chocolate milkshake.

"You all right?" he asked.

"Yeah, I'm okay, but I don't want to go on any more rides."

"Let's go down to the beach."

Brent raced me to the water, and, without thinking about it, we both dived in with all our clothes on. I'd never been swimming at night before, and the water felt different. Smoother. How could you explain that? In the distance you couldn't see where the water ended and the sky began. It made the world seem bigger than usual. Of course, it was the middle of the city, so you couldn't see any stars. But I knew they were up there. Swimming at night reminds you that there are stars up there.

When we got out, Brent wrote "Marty" in the sand like a graffiti artist's tag on the subway. I wrote "Brendan Peter Conrad, Esquire" in curlicue script. *What am I doing here?* I thought. I looked at Brent. He was staring at me. I stared back. I didn't know what was going to happen.

"Let's take a walk," Brent said.

We walked along the beach. No one was around. When we got tired, we sat on the sand. My clothes were still damp, and the breeze off the water made me shiver a little bit.

"You cold?" Brent asked, and without waiting for me to answer he started to rub my arms and back, the way my mom used to rub me down with a towel when I was little and would stay in the water too long and come out with lips blue and teeth chattering.

"Are you cold, honey?" she'd ask, and I'd always say "No!" because I didn't want her to give me a lecture about staying in the water too long. Then she'd smile and rub me with a towel till I stopped shivering.

Brent was rubbing me that way, vigorously, but the goose bumps didn't go away. It was the first time he'd touched me since the night he put his hand on the back of my neck. Brent stopped rubbing and pulled me close, so my head was resting on his chest.

"Marty, Marty, Marty." He let go a little and tipped my face back and looked at me. Then he kissed me.

Of course, I could have stopped him. I could have said, "I can't do this. We better go home." But I didn't. I let him kiss me.

Brent was the one who whispered, "It's late. I better take you home."

I nodded. Then he kissed my neck. "You taste like potato chips," he said. He kept kissing me. Kissing and licking. "I love salt," he whispered. He pulled up my T-shirt and licked my belly. It tickled, and I shrieked and rolled over out of his reach. Brent tackled me, and we rolled over in the sand, over and over and over, laughing. When we stopped, Brent was lying on top of me, and when he kissed me this time, something funny happened. All these parts started jumping around inside me that I never even knew I had. I knew what was going on. I'm not that dumb, even if I am a virgin.

In the subway, on the way home, I leaned my head on Brent's chest and he stroked my hair. I don't know if he noticed, but I was crying a little bit because I love Rob, and my hand was missing his, even while my insides were wanting Brent.

Safe

The next day it was raining. I knew the guys wouldn't be playing ball in the park. Sometimes they played if it was just a drizzle, but this was a steady downpour that started early in the moring and didn't stop for the rest of the day.

I wanted to see Rob. I wanted to hold his hand and feel his arms around me. I had to know he was real and what happened with Brent the night before was just a dream.

I moped around the house all morning, rearranging things in my room. Then I walked over to Grandma's. When I appeared in her hallway, dripping wet, Grandma said, "Have you ever heard of an umbrella?"

"Don't worry," I said. "I'm not going to melt."

"I'm not worried about you. I'm worried about my

kitchen floor, which I just mopped yesterday."

By that point I was dripping onto the linoleum in front of the refrigerator as I fished around for something to eat.

"Help yourself," Grandma muttered.

I found some roast beef and pickles and made myself a sandwich. While I was eating, I didn't say a word to Grandma. In fact, I glared at her every time she came into the room.

Finally she said, "Did you come over for a visit, or wasn't there any food at your house?"

That's when I started to cry. Grandma sat down next to me.

"All right, grumpy. Tell me what's wrong."

"It's raining!" I wailed.

Grandma nodded, as if anyone could see what a terrible tragedy this was.

"It's raining," I said again for emphasis. "Which means that Rob won't be at the park playing baseball. Which means I won't get to see him."

Grandma patted my hand. "So you'll see him tomorrow," she said gently. "Maybe you'll live till tomorrow?"

"But what if it rains tomorrow? And the next day. And the next. Sometimes it rains for a whole week."

"And sometimes it clears up the next day, Miss Optimism."

"Grandma," I whispered, "I *have* to see him today."

Grandma understood. Maybe it's because of Baldy. Maybe there are times when she's doing the laundry or reading a magazine and suddenly she just *has* to run her hand over his bald head. Being in love is like that.

"Call him up, honey. You can meet him somewhere else. You don't have to go to the park. In my day we used to meet at the soda fountain and order one cherry Coke with two straws."

"I can't call him." I started to cry again.

"Why not?"

"Because his parents don't approve of him having a girlfriend. They say he's too young."

Grandma was quiet for a while, thinking that over.

"Why don't you go over to the park?" Grandma said finally. "If he knows you can't call, maybe he'll come looking for you."

"No. I know he won't be there, and then I'll just feel worse."

I went into the living room and turned on the TV and the radio. I turned down the volume on the TV so I could listen to music while I watched "Days of Our Lives." Michael Jackson was singing "The kid is not my son," which was perfect background music for a soap opera. Besides, you don't need the sound to figure out what's going on in those shows.

After half an hour, Grandma came in and turned off the radio.

"Marty," she said, "for God's sake go to the park."

I didn't go directly to the baseball field. I took the long way around through the park. I was happy to see I wasn't the only idiot out in the rain. There were quite a few people jogging with rain dripping down their foreheads into their eyes. Dedicated joggers don't care what the weather's like.

I didn't see Rob at first because he was standing under a tree trying to keep out of the rain. Then he ran toward me, waving.

"Hey, what took you so long? I'm getting drenched out here waiting for you."

"I didn't think you'd be here," I said.

"Why not?"

"Because I knew you wouldn't be playing today."

"So what? You think I only meet you here because I happen to be playing baseball?"

I felt really dumb. But happy at the same time. I must have looked like a goof, grinning and guilty and dripping wet. All of a sudden Rob laughed.

"Come on," he said. "Let's get out of the rain."

I followed him to the shed. It wasn't exactly the best shelter. Rain was pouring through the hole in the roof, and the ground was muddy, but if we sat on the junk piled against the walls, we could stay out of the rain and the mud.

"It would be easier if I could call you," I said, as I perched on the side of an old wheelbarrow.

"I know, Marty." Rob sat down next to me. "But it wouldn't be worth it. Believe me."

"Why? What would your parents do if they found out?"

"First, Dad would probably sit me down and have a serious talk. He'd tell me that I'm still very young and haven't developed the maturity to handle the complicated physical and emotional aspects of a love relationship. Then he would stress the importance of using this period of my life to develop my mind and my body through academics and sports and remind me again that both he and my mother would prefer for me to attend a private boys' school, preferably Catholic."

"All right, so you get a lecture. Everybody gets lectured once in a while."

"That's just step one. After a couple of weeks, if the whole thing hadn't blown over, Dad would put his foot down and send me to Connecticut to spend the summer with my grandparents. Mom might try to step in and suggest that he was being a little harsh, but Dad would say that it was for my own good and I would thank him for it later."

"What if you refused to go? What if you ran off with your girlfriend instead and didn't tell them where you were?"

Rob shook his head. "I'd never do that," he said. "Dad knows that."

We were both quiet for a few minutes, listening to the rain.

"How long do you think we have?" I asked.

"What do you mean?"

"Till this blows over."

Some people might have thought I was talking about the rain. But I knew Rob would understand. He reached out and pulled me over so I was sitting on his lap. He's strong. I could feel the muscles of his legs supporting me, his arms around me, the fresh rain smell of wet earth and grass surrounding us. Rob held my head against his neck and whispered in my ear, "You don't know me very well, Marty. When I love somebody, it doesn't blow over. Not soon. Not ever."

I closed my eyes and let my whole body relax, knowing I'd made it home. Safe.

Racing, Slowing Down

I tried to avoid Brent. I didn't know what else to do. I knew if I went to the abandoned building and sat on the tattered mattress with him, I'd want him to kiss me. I wanted him to kiss me all the time, whether I went or not.

Brent still showed up at the park, but he was quiet. He didn't tell us funny stories, and he didn't flirt with me. Rob had to notice. But he probably thought Brent was having trouble at home. Brent's parents are both some kind of hotshot professionals, and, according to Brent, they can't stand each other. But they both agree on one thing—Brent is wasting his potential. I guess they don't think that drawing comics counts for much. Brent says it's his life, and if he wants to waste it, he will. But sometimes he just can't take listening to his mom and dad criticizing him all the time. So, he goes and holes up in the abandoned building for a few days. His parents don't know where he is, and when he goes back things are even worse, but he says it's worth it because he's got to have a break from them. Rob probably figured it was one of those times.

I called Annie and asked her to meet me at the playground. I wanted to sit on the swings and have her tell me again that I shouldn't see Brent. But she said she was busy. When I called the next day, she was still busy. I asked her what was going on, and she told me her mom was sick and she had to help out at home. I offered to go over and keep her company, but she said her mom needed to rest and didn't want any extra people around.

The next night I didn't even call her. I called Grandma, but of course she wasn't home. I hung up the phone.

"Dad, do you think Grandma's gonna marry Baldy?" I asked.

"Gee, I don't know. Maybe."

"Well, what do you think of him?"

"He seems like a decent sort of person."

"She's your mother. Don't you think you should take more of an interest?"

"Uh-huh." He wasn't listening.

"Do you want to play Scrabble?" I asked. "Or gin rummy?"

"Not right now, Marty. I'm reading the paper."

I went to find Mom. She was ironing her uniform, getting ready for work the next day.

"You want me to do that?" I asked her.

She looked up, surprised.

"Thanks, honey, but I'm almost done."

I put on some lotion that she had on a table beside her bed.

"Can I have this? I like the way it smells."

"I guess so. Is something wrong, Marty?"

"No."

"Why don't you go over and see Annie?"

"Her mom's sick and doesn't want any 'extra people' around."

"Oh." Mom went in the bathroom and brushed her teeth.

"Can you believe that?" I said. But I knew she couldn't hear me with the water running.

The phone rang, and I went into my room to answer it. A man with an Irish accent asked to speak to Martha. I told him he had the wrong number.

"Wrong number? No, no. It be Martha's house. I'm sure of it. There's a young lady, you see, who pretends her name be Marty, but I know . . ."

I started to laugh.

"Oh," I said. "If it isn't Brendan Peter Conrad himself! To what do I owe this great honor?"

"You?! Are you the very Martha of which I've been speaking?"

"I guess so," I answered. "Because I *have* been thinking that my name was Marty."

"What a pity. What a pity. And Martha be such a lovely name."

"Hi, Brent."

"Hi, Marty." He dropped the accent.

"What's up?"

"I've got an idea."

"What is it?"

"A surprise. Can you meet me at the playground near your house in ten minutes?"

"I don't know. I'm not sure it's—"

"I won't touch you. I promise. I won't even get within six feet of you. You'll see! So, don't worry, kid. Just be there in ten minutes. And bring your roller skates."

He hung up before I could answer. Bring my roller skates? He must have known curiosity would overcome all moral considerations.

Brent arrived on his friend Jimmy's motorcycle.

"Put on your skates. I'm going to take you for a ride," he said, as he unwound a thick rope and tied it to the back of the bike.

"You have got to be kidding!"

"No. You said you like to move. This'll be amazing. Better than the subway. Better than the Cyclone, even."

"I'll get killed."

"No, you won't. I'll be careful. I won't go too fast . . . unless you want me to!" He arched his eyebrows.

"No. That's all right," I said.

"There's no danger," he continued. "You're not attached. If you get scared, just let go of the rope."

I must have looked a little tense, because as Brent handed me the rope, he added, "Relax. It'll be fun."

Brent was right. It was fun. He started out going slow, slower even than I go when I'm skating by myself. So, I got used to it and learned to bend my knees and lean back a little and shift my weight with the movements of the bike.

"Ready for a little speed?" Brent asked.

"I think so."

We took off in a burst, like a race. But we could go fast for only a few feet before Brent started slowing down because there was a Stop sign at every corner, and, if he waited to brake till the last minute, I would go flying.

We went on like that for a while—racing, slowing down, racing, slowing down. My heart was pounding. I didn't have time to get too scared before he slowed down again.

After about ten blocks Brent stopped the bike and turned around to face me.

"How're you doing?" he asked.

"Great!" My cheeks were burning. My whole body felt hot.

"Had enough for tonight?"

I nodded, even though part of me wanted to go on like that forever. I wished we could ride on a straight, empty road, roaring down it, on and on with no one around and the wind rushing past. I wished I still had long hair so it could fly out behind me and whip around my face. On a straight, wide, empty road, I would forget about everything except the wind and the sky and the bike and Brent. On a straight, empty road, far away, outside the city, I could lean back and see the stars rushing by.

But I was stuck in the city. There was traffic everywhere. It would be too dangerous to go fast.

Brent untied the rope, and I climbed on behind him. The skates made my feet feel heavy. I was tired. I put my arms all the way around Brent and rested my head against his back as he drove me home.

When we got to the playground, I swung one skate-heavy foot over the bike and slid off. Brent stayed where he was, gripping the handlebars.

"Did you have a good time?" He smiled at me.

"Yeah." I stood beside the bike, tracing the outline of the seat with my finger, praying he would kiss me. But he kept his promise.

Two to One

Brent was grinning when I saw him at the park the next day.

"Let's play some ball," he said to me and Rob when the game ended. "Just the three of us. Marty can take both of us on, don't you think, Robbie?"

I haven't played much baseball, and no matter how many times I remind myself to keep my eye on the ball, I always have this impulse to duck at the last moment.

Rob and Brent let me have as many strikes as I needed.

"It's only fair because it's two against one," Brent said.

Rob was pitching, so Brent squatted behind home plate, returning the ball. I could feel him watching me.

From the pitcher's mound, Rob yelled tips to me on how to stand and how to hold the bat. It didn't help.

"Strike seventeen," Brent called out. "She's going for *The Guinness Book of World Records*."

"I quit," I said. "I'll never get it."

"Keep trying," Rob said. "You'll get it eventually. It just takes practice."

Brent got up and stood behind me. He wrapped his arms around me and closed his hands over mine, gripping the bat.

"Relax," Brent whispered. "I'm going to help you." He didn't need to tell me to relax. My whole body went limp, and I couldn't breathe. As the ball hurtled toward us, I felt the power of Brent's swing flow right through me to the bat.

The jolt of the bat hitting the ball caught me by surprise. Then Rob was running toward the outfield as the ball hurtled past him.

For a second Brent kept his arms wrapped around me. Then he gave me a little shove in the direction of first base and said, "Go on. Run."

Brent and Rob let me get a home run, tossing the ball back and forth between them, dropping it, bungling on purpose. I ran as if my life depended on it. When I left third base, Brent was chasing me, holding the ball out in front of him. I slid into home plate as Brent tackled me and threw me to the ground.

"What is this?!" I was gasping for breath, so I could hardly get the words out. "Tackle baseball?"

"*Safe!!!*" shouted Rob. He reached out and pulled me to my feet. "Congratulations!" he said, and picked me up, twirling me around and around. "What do you say we quit while we're ahead?" Rob offered when he set me down. "Marty's game. One to nothing!"

Brent was still lying in the dirt by home plate. "Oh," he moaned, writhing on the ground as if in great pain. "It hurts so bad to lose."

A Prayer

That evening after the baseball game, I waited for Brent at the playground. I knew he'd show up. He rode Jimmy's motorcycle right up on the sidewalk and into the playground. All the mothers and fathers probably glared at him, but I don't know for sure because I was looking at Brent. He was wearing sunglasses even though it was after seven in the evening, and he had his cigarettes rolled into the sleeve of his T-shirt the way they used to do in the fifties.

"Hey, little girl. You wanna go for a ride? I'll give you a piece of candy."

"I don't like candy."

"I'll give you something even better."

"What is it?"

"Can't tell you. It's a surprise."

"I love surprises," I said, and got on behind him.

"Where are we going?" I asked.

"I don't know. Where do you want to go?"

I considered for a minute.

"California," I decided.

"Cool. But I'm not one hundred percent sure I can get you home by nine-thirty, even if I drive super fast."

"That could be a problem."

"Would you settle for Staten Island?"

"What's there to see on Staten Island?"

"Nothing. You don't go for Staten Island. You go to ride the ferry. Ferries are amazing."

"If you say so."

"I do."

We rode the ferry. As we stood up front, the wind blew in our faces; it was different from the wind that rushes past when you ride a motorcycle. I could feel the water out there, tiny little drops on my skin.

Brent stood close beside me so our arms were touching as we leaned over the side of the boat.

"Brent?"

He turned to me and put his finger on my lips.

"Shh! Don't talk," he said.

Then he kissed me. When Brent kisses me I don't want him to stop. Even though I know it's wrong.

Every morning for the next two weeks, I told myself that I wouldn't see Brent anymore. But every evening I went to meet him at the abandoned building. I couldn't even think about what would happen if Rob ever found out. Besides the fact that I was cheating on him with his best friend, Rob would probably think that what Brent and I did was a sin. We never took our clothes off, and we didn't have real sex, but I doubt if that distinction would mean much to Rob.

I tried to imagine Rob angry, but it was impossible. He was teaching me to play baseball. After that day we played with Brent, Rob and I practiced every day. It was Rob's idea. He never got tired of pitching to me, letting me try over and over and over until I got it.

Brent didn't come to the park much. He'd stop by every few days to say hi to Rob, but he never stayed long. I could hardly stand it when he was there. Sometimes I'd catch him staring at me, and I'd look away really fast.

Rob never seemed to notice, though. He was always happy when Brent was with us and wanted him to stay longer. One day when Brent showed up, Rob said, "Hey, buddy, stick around. I want you to see how much progress Marty's made."

I was so embarrassed, I forgot everything I'd learned and couldn't hit the ball at all.

Rob came over to me. "Don't worry, Marty," he said. "This is not the tryouts for the major leagues. It's only Brent."

"Just pretend I'm not here," Brent called out from where he was watching. Very funny.

I finally settled down and started hitting. I was doing really well, hitting almost every one. Brent cheered and whistled. All of a sudden I burst into tears. Rob came running over.

"What's the matter?"

"Nothing."

Brent watched from a few feet away. Rob put his arm around me.

"You're doing great, Marty. You're getting the hang of it. A couple more weeks and we'll put you on the team."

I kept crying. I knew he wanted to comfort me, but I couldn't even tell him what was wrong.

Brent came over and said, "Look, I better get going." Then he squeezed my arm. "Take it easy, Marty." I nodded without looking at him, and he walked away.

Rob and I started walking. I dragged the bat behind me in the dirt. We walked over to the shed. I hadn't been there since the day it had rained. It's a special place to Rob. Not an everyday place. We dropped down through the hole in the roof and sat against the wall. Rob was quiet, waiting for me to explain. I wanted to. I wanted to tell him about Brent. I wanted Rob to understand that it didn't mean I loved him less. But I wasn't even sure I understood myself.

The silence crept between us.

"What am I supposed to do?" I asked. "Pray?"

I didn't look at him because I didn't want to see the hurt on his face.

"Well? Isn't that what you do when you come here?"

"Sometimes."

"I've never prayed. I don't know how."

"Yes, you do. You just don't call it that."

"Why don't you teach me how to pray? If you can teach me to play baseball, I bet you can teach me how to pray."

"You just talk to God. Tell Him how you feel. That's all."

I was willing to try. After all, I didn't seem to have anyone else to talk to. But every time I tried to tell God that I needed help, that I wanted to do the right thing, I kept seeing Brent's face, the way it looked with the gash over his eye, scrunched up in pain, begging me to go be with him.

I squeezed both hands between my knees and stared down at them.

"Rob . . ." I said. "How come you never kiss me?"

I didn't look at him. But I could feel the space between us again. The space with God in it.

"I don't think God would mind if you kissed me," I said.

Rob didn't answer.

"Would He?"

"No," he said. I turned to look at him. He seemed so far away and scared. I started thinking maybe it wasn't God he was scared of. Maybe he was scared because he didn't know what to do. I'm pretty sure Rob hasn't had much experience with girls.

The thing is that if it hadn't been for Brent, I wouldn't have known what to do, either, and who knows what would have happened? But, however wrong it might be, Brent did teach me how to touch someone. So when Rob sat there all stiff and frozen, I moved in real, real close and kissed him. I could tell he liked it. Our mouths had never been together like that, and our hands and bodies got jealous, so we started touching in all the places we had never dared touch before.

Rob stood up suddenly and turned away from me. "Don't, Marty." His back was to me. And all of a sudden I was sitting there alone, where just a moment before I was connected to Rob. I felt like I was going to die.

"I love you, Rob," I said to his back.

Rob turned around slowly and looked at me. His face was blank. I had no idea what he was thinking. I wanted to jump up and hoist myself out through the hole in the roof.

Then Rob lunged toward me like something breaking—a jar of jelly beans, and everything poured out, hard and sweet and full of bright colors. He buried his head somewhere in the middle of me, clutching on to me. I pulled his face up and kissed him again. Then we sank down on the ground and held on to each other very, very tight.

That evening as I was walking home, it wasn't just my hand that was missing Rob, but the whole length of my body.

Leave Me Alone

After that time in the shed with Rob, I knew I couldn't keep meeting Brent at night. But I didn't know how to tell him. I had to baby-sit for the Morrisons that night, so I thought at least I wouldn't have to face Brent till the next day.

Mr. Morrison dropped me off and waited till I got inside the building. As I started up the stairs, someone tapped on the glass door. I spun around, frightened. It was Brent. I opened the door.

"What are you doing here?" I asked.

"Are you okay?"

"Yeah."

He reached out to touch me.

"It's late, Brent. I have to go upstairs."

"I know. I just wanted to see you for a minute. I

couldn't stand to see you crying and not be able to hold you."

His fingers were sneaking around my face and neck. I had to clench up all my insides so they wouldn't want him to touch me.

"Marty?"

"What?"

"What's the matter?"

"Nothing." I know I should have had the guts to tell him, but I couldn't.

"You don't want me here, do you?" I hated to see his face crumple up like that.

"No," I whispered.

Brent's hand dropped to his side. He turned and walked away. I followed him.

"Brent . . ." He ignored me and kept walking. Then, without any warning, he kicked a parking meter. Then another. And another. He took some of those big plastic garbage cans and hurled them across the street. I didn't say anything. It was a hot night, and there were other people on the street. They stared at us as they walked by. Brent was lashing out at anything that got in his way. Sometimes, when there was nothing else, he slammed his fist against the brick wall of an apartment building. I knew it must have hurt like hell, but I didn't try to stop him.

I kept hoping he would calm down. Instead, it got worse. He was crazy, beating his fists on the hoods of cars and throwing anything he found in the street against the sides of buildings. Empty Coke cans. A piece of rusted tailpipe. A half-rotten orange. I thought maybe if I could talk to him, it would help. All I had a chance to say was "Brent . . ." before he whirled around with his arm flung out and stopped himself before he hit me. He stood there and stared at me with his fist clenched. He was much more frightened than I was. Then he ran.

I ran after him. I didn't think I would be able to keep up with him, but my legs are really strong from skating so much. And Brent isn't in such good shape. So, I was right behind him when he hurled himself down the stairs of the subway station. He stumbled at the bottom, but he still got ahead of me because I came down the stairs much more cautiously. I saw him jump over the turnstile and disappear into the station.

There was nobody in the booth where they sell tokens. In fact, there was nobody else in the station, so I climbed over, too. By the time I caught up with him, Brent had found some bottles that were lying on the platform and was smashing them against the tracks. It was worse than Coke cans and oranges. I started shaking when I heard the glass shattering. Maybe I should be used to that kind of thing growing up in the city, but the truth is that I'm squeamish when it comes to violence. I don't even like to see violent movies. But I had made up my mind I wasn't going to leave him alone. No matter what.

When there were no more bottles left, Brent stopped and stood with his back to me. I went over and touched his arm. My hand was shaking, and I couldn't make any words come out, but I wanted him to know I was still there.

He wouldn't turn around and look at me, but when he shouted, it echoed through the whole station. "Leave me alone. Don't you know when you're not wanted? Now get out! *Get out!*" Then he doubled over and held on to himself and sobbed. I peeled his arms away from his body and wrapped my own around him. We both sank down onto the subway platform, and I held him.

We sat in the empty subway station for a long time. Little by little I could feel Brent's body relax. He was close to me, and I felt him breathing. We didn't talk.

When I got home, my parents were completely hysterical. It had gotten so late, Dad decided to call the Morrisons, and Mr. Morrison told him he'd seen me safely inside at ten-thirty. Then Dad called Annie, Grandma, and finally the police. He lost his temper when the police told him there was nothing they could do, and that he should go in to file a missing-person's report if I didn't turn up. Mom woke up when she heard Dad yelling at the police officer.

It takes a lot to get my father mad, but I had definitely gone over the limit. He said enough was enough—he had stayed out of my business and trusted me, but now I had better tell him what I was up to.

Mom just kept saying over and over, "Where have you been, Marty? I want you to tell me where you've been."

I knew they deserved an explanation. But I couldn't talk to them. Where would I begin?

"It doesn't matter. It's all over. So forget about it." I thought I sounded calm. But when I went to my room, I slammed the door and burst into tears.

Dad followed me and knocked on my door.

"Marty?"

"What?"

"Can I come in?"

"No."

"I want to talk to you."

"I can't. Please, Dad. I'll talk to you tomorrow. I promise."

"All right, Marty. It'll wait till tomorrow. Good night."

I cried myself to sleep, but quietly, so they couldn't hear me.

Lessons

I never thought I would look forward to going back to school, but I decided anything would be better than these last two weeks of vacation. I never did tell my parents where I was that night. The next day I stayed in my room, pretending to be asleep, until I heard my father leave for work. I didn't want to talk to him until I'd had a chance to sort things out. I wanted to ride the subway all day and think about everything that had happened the day before. I wanted to think about lying close to Rob in the shed and about Brent sobbing in my arms and about how I felt about all of it.

I didn't make it to the subway, though. As I left my building, there was Rob, sitting on the steps. He had never been to my house before. It was so strange to see him there that for a second I had the feeling I didn't know him.

Rob jumped up. "I've been waiting for you," he said.

"Why didn't you ring the bell?"

"I don't know," he muttered. "I just thought . . . it would be better to talk out here." The red crept up Rob's neck to his face, and it occurred to me that he didn't want to be alone with me in our apartment with my parents at work.

"Look, Marty . . . I . . . I just wanted to talk to you. About yesterday."

I felt my stomach wrench. I wondered if somehow he knew about me and Brent. I imagined it splashed across the front page of the newspaper—YOUNG MAN VANDALIZES SUBWAY STATION WHEN GIRL JILTS HIM. Maybe the whole city was reading about it on the way to work.

Or, more likely, Brent had called up and told Rob. To get back at me. To hurt me.

I was waiting for Rob to start yelling at me, telling me I was a slut, a cheat, and a liar. Instead, he said, very quietly, "We shouldn't have done that yesterday."

I wanted to cry. I bit my bottom lip so hard I could taste the slight metal taste of blood.

"Oh," I said.

"Well, what do *you* think?" Rob asked.

I didn't want to look at him. "I have to go see my grandmother," I said. I tried to walk past him.

Rob put his hand on my arm. "Marty."

"What?"

"Tell me what you're thinking."

"I liked it." I said it so quietly that you could probably barely hear me over the noise of the city streets, but I looked him right in the eye.

Rob looked away. "I liked it, too," he said. "But it's not right."

I wanted to touch him the way I had in the shed, pulling him gently back to me. But we were standing on the steps to my apartment building. And besides, he seemed too far away, out of my reach. I didn't know what to do.

"Is there something in your religion that says it's wrong to touch people?" I asked.

"No."

"Then, why can't we—?"

Rob turned back to me. When he spoke, I felt as if he had grabbed me by the shoulders and was shaking me, even though he didn't touch me.

"Don't you get it, Marty? Ever since yesterday all I can think about is how it felt to hold you. I want to. Don't you understand? I want to. But I can't."

I could feel it. Whatever it was that came rushing out of him when he reached out for me in the shed. It was just below the surface, barely under control. And I knew Rob was afraid of it. Afraid that he couldn't control it.

We'll be careful, I wanted to say. *We'll be careful. And I'll go to a clinic, just in case.* But I knew that wouldn't help.

Rob was leaning against the wall of my building with

his arms across his chest. The space was all around him, and I couldn't reach through. The only thing I could think of, the only way I could help him, was to leave him alone.

"Grandma and Baldy are renting a house on the beach for a month," I said. "I told her I'd stop by to say good-bye."

Rob nodded. "Will I see you this afternoon?" he asked.

"Yeah, sure," I said. "Unless I decide to elope with Grandma and Baldy."

Rob almost smiled. "Marty," he said as I turned to go, "I'm sorry."

Grandma was busy packing, but she dropped an armful of plastic dishes on the floor and squeezed me right into her big, soft bosom.

"Oh, Marty! I was worried sick when your father called last night. Are you all right?"

I couldn't breathe too well, so I squirmed out of her arms and started picking up plastic plates.

"Where do you want these?"

"In the picnic basket. Marty, what happened? Where were you?"

"I don't want to talk about it. Okay, Grandma?"

"Oh." She squatted down and scooped up the plastic silverware and the checkered tablecloth. "Doesn't want to talk about it," she muttered.

"It's kind of complicated," I said.

"Complicated. I see. Well, as long as you're all

right. . . . Come in the bedroom. You can help me decide what clothes to take."

I followed her into the bedroom and hunkered down on the bed.

"I wonder if it gets cool in the evenings. What do you think? Should I take this heavy sweater?"

"Yeah, sure. It can't hurt to have it. Just in case."

"I suppose so . . ."

"Grandma, can I go with you?"

She sat down next to me.

"Marty, are you in some kind of trouble? You can tell me."

"No. It's just that I've been in this lousy, stinking city all summer. We never go anywhere."

"Your mother gets so little vacation time. It's not her fault."

"I know that. But what am I supposed to do all summer? A person could go crazy."

"You know I'd love to have you. It's just that this is the first time Joe and I have gone away together. It's not a good time. You could come next summer! Assuming everything goes well." She winked at me.

"Never mind. It doesn't matter. Mom and Dad probably wouldn't let me go anyway."

"Maybe you could come out for a couple of days once we're settled. I'm sure there's a bus. We could pick you up at the station. How does that sound?"

"I don't know. Maybe . . ."

"Sure. That's what we'll do. It'll be fun." Grandma

stood up and stuffed the big sweater into her suitcase. "You're right," she said. "It can't hurt to have it."

Dinner was silent. Mom and Dad didn't ask me any more questions about where I'd been. I knew they were waiting for me to tell them. I mashed my peas into a paste with my fork.

"Marty," Mom said, "please don't play with your food. If you don't want it, leave it alone."

"I do want it. I'm making mashed peas. If people can eat mashed potatoes, why not mashed peas?"

"Are you planning to eat them?"

"Maybe. It depends—if they're good." I reached for the salt and pepper. "I think they need seasoning."

Mom stood up. "I can't take this," she said, and went into her room.

"Marty, your mother is very upset about what happened last night."

"Sorry."

"It would help if you would talk to her, if you would tell her where you were."

I kept mashing my peas.

"All right, Marty," Dad continued. "I can't force you to talk to us. I wish you felt that you could, and if you change your mind, we're here. You know that, right?"

I nodded without looking up from my peas.

"Your mother and I discussed this last night, and we decided that you've had too much freedom. We don't want you going out after supper anymore."

"Ever?"

"For the rest of vacation. After that you should be home in the evenings anyway, doing your homework."

"Dad! You know I—"

"Marty. There's nothing to discuss. This is not negotiable."

"What about baby-sitting? Can I still go baby-sitting?"

"No, Martini. We don't feel we can trust you. I'm sorry."

I'm allowed to go out during the day, so I can still meet Rob in the park. We've gone back to the way things were before, and neither of us ever mentions what happened. I thought I would be angry and hurt all the time, but mostly I feel sad. I love Rob more than ever. I just wish I could figure out how to reach through that terrible space around him.

I miss Grandma. And Annie. And Brent. I wish Brent would call. I know he won't, though. He's too proud. Besides, he probably hates me.

I'm sure Dad thinks I'm moping around the house because I'm grounded. He always feels terrible when he has to punish me, so he's trying to make up for it any way he can. Every night he brings home something special for dinner. Ice cream or pizza, or mu-shu shrimp from my favorite Chinese restaurant. After dinner we watch TV or play Scrabble.

Mom doesn't think it's right to be too nice to someone who's being punished. She's still mad because I won't tell them where I was that night. I heard her arguing with my father one night when they thought I was asleep.

"You don't have to pamper her, Harry," she said. "It weakens the point."

I guess I'm supposed to learn a lesson. The trouble is, I don't know what lesson I'm supposed to learn. I wish I could tell Mom where I was that night, but I know it would be even worse if she knew. She would never understand how I feel about Brent.

Every night when I'm washing the dishes and Mom is putting away the food, I want to tell her that the only lesson I've learned so far is that sometimes you get into situations where no matter what you do, you are going to hurt someone.

Classmates

Ever since school started, I am home every evening doing my homework. Mom is very pleased. She probably thinks I've learned that lesson I was supposed to learn. The truth is, I have nothing else to do. Annie's still mad at me. When I told her I stopped seeing Brent, she just said "It's about time," and walked away. Grandma is still at the beach with Baldy. I figure they'll probably elope without me and never come back. And Rob is busy doing hours and hours of homework every day. His parents expect him to make the honor roll every term. But it isn't just that. He actually enjoys it.

Rob is in my English class. He knows everything, and he's always raising his hand. Usually he brings up philosophical points about an individual's rights and responsibilities in society. Rob is very concerned about how human beings treat one another. Our teacher always says that Rob raises the discussion to a higher level. That's for sure. When Rob feels strongly about something, his face gets red, and he stammers. I sit next to him and hold my breath until he gets the words out. Sometimes I can hear someone snicker in the back of the class. It's definitely not cool to care too much. I feel bad for Rob, but it doesn't seem to bother him. He has some inner sense of what's right, and he doesn't care that much what other people think of him. Still, I wish I could stick up for him the way Brent did. I bet Brent's been doing that for years. But I don't have the nerve.

In English class I think about these moral issues. In math class I'm just trying to survive. Annie is in my class. The first day she sat next to me as if we were still friends. Then Mr. Farley took attendance. When he read Brent's name, Annie turned and glared at me as if I'd purposely arranged to be in the same class with him.

Brent didn't come to class that day, but I was a wreck anyway. For the rest of the period I didn't hear a thing Mr. Farley said. I spent the whole time plotting how I could convince my guidance counselor to switch me to another math class.

"I just don't like the class," I told Mr. Gellman.

"Mr. Farley is considered one of the best teachers in the school, Marty. Give it a few more days. I can't go switching everyone's schedule around because they 'don't like the class.' "

"I know. But I won't learn any math if I stay in that class. I know I won't."

"Do me a favor and give it a few more days. If you still feel this way at the end of the week, check back with me."

The end of the week! I knew I'd never make it to the end of the week. That night I told my parents I was dropping math.

"Why?" my mother asked.

"I want to do really well in my other subjects this year. And I only need two years of math to graduate. Why do I have to take it now? I've got two more years of high school after this."

Dad put his hand on my shoulder.

"Trouble is, Martini, you underestimate yourself. You can handle four majors if you put your mind to it. Give it a try, okay?"

For the next two days Brent didn't show up in class, but I couldn't concentrate. I never knew when he might walk through the door. It would be just like Brent to come halfway into the period. I wasn't learning any math. I felt bad because Mr. Farley is really cool. He puts a problem on the board, and then he whips around, fast, points his finger at someone, and says, "Pete!" It's like a quiz show. If you get the wrong answer, he says, "Sorry, Mr. Gomez, you do not win the home-entertainment center. Anyone else want to try?"

Hands shoot up all over the room. Everyone wants him to notice them. Even Annie has become a math whiz. But when he calls on me, I get the buzzer every time. I know Annie is disgusted with me.

I told Rob that Brent was supposed to be in my math class, but I hadn't seen him yet. Rob said that Brent never comes to school the first week because he thinks it's a waste of time. All they do is "pass out books and get to know each other." At the end of the first week, Rob and I were standing on the corner in front of the school, waiting for the light to change. Brent came up behind us and put an arm around each of us.

"Hey, guys, what's happening? How's school?"

"Not bad," Rob answered.

"Did I miss anything?"

Rob grinned. "Not unless you wanted a book this year."

"No, thanks. Did any cute girls move to town while I wasn't looking?"

"Marty's in your math class. She's cute."

Brent pinched me. "Yeah. Marty's real cute. But she's taken, buddy-boy."

The light changed and we crossed the street. Brent didn't go into the school with us, though. He saw some of his friends heading down the street, and he took off in their direction.

"Catch you guys later," he said.

I wasn't sure if Brent ever came to school that day. He wasn't around at lunch, but Rob said he usually left school at lunchtime even though it's not allowed. I had math right after lunch. Brent caught up with me outside room 306.

"Is this it?"

"Yeah."

He walked in and looked around. Mr. Farley wasn't there yet. I sat down next to Annie, in the third row. Brent came over to me.

"This is too close," he said.

"What?"

"You're sitting too close to the front."

"This is Annie," I said. "Annie, Brent."

Brent took his time, looking Annie up and down, checking her out. "So this is Annie," he said finally, approving and seductive at the same time. I wanted to kill him. Annie made a face and opened her math book to check her homework.

Brent sat down next to me as Mr. Farley walked in. Mr. Farley had on sunglasses and his hair was slicked back like a greaser from the fifties. He sat down in an empty seat in the front row and said, "Where's the teacher of this dumb class anyway?" He punched the guy sitting next to him lightly on the arm. "What I can't figure out is why the hell I gotta learn math. I ain't gonna use it." Everybody was laughing. Mr. Farley continued. "I bet I could teach this class. There's nothin' to it. Teachers think they're so smart, but anybody can teach math." He got up, went to the front of the room, picked up a piece of chalk, and said, "Yeah. I'm gonna teach this stinkin' class."

"Why don't you grow up, Farley?"

Mr. Farley pushed the sunglasses up on the top of his head and looked at Brent.

"Well, well. If it isn't Brent Conrad. What happened— did you get lost on your way to the police station?"

Everyone laughed. Except Brent, of course. And me. Brent unfolded a piece of paper. It was the only thing on his desk. He didn't have a notebook or textbook or even a pencil. He read from the paper.

"Math Two. Farley. Room three-oh-six. Ain't I in the right place?"

"You got everything right except the date, Conrad. All right, class, turn to page forty-seven. Let's go over the homework. Any questions? Problems?"

Mr. Farley was all business for the rest of the class. I didn't understand the homework, but I didn't ask any questions. Brent doodled on the desk, and Mr. Farley ignored him. At the end of class, Brent was the first one out the door. I ran to catch up with him.

"Aren't you going to get a book?"

"I hate that guy."

"He's not that bad. I think he's sort of—"

"Shut up, Marty. You don't know what you're talking about." He turned and ran down the stairs, leaving me standing in the middle of the hall.

When I went back to Mr. Gellman, he offered to set up a meeting with me and Mr. Farley. He said he couldn't justify transferring me out without a valid reason, but if there was a problem, he was sure Mr. Farley would try to help.

We met during my free period Monday morning.

"Marty seems to be having some kind of problem in your class, Tom," Mr. Gellman explained.

"I want to drop math," I blurted out, "but my parents won't let me."

"Why do you want to drop math?" Mr. Farley asked.

"I'm lost. It's only the second week, and I'm already lost."

"How about coming after school for some help?"

"After school? I can't come after school!" That was the only time I got to see Rob, before he went home to study.

"Do you have a job?"

"No. But I can't come."

"All right, Marty. I'd like to help you. I'll tell you what. Let's meet at this time for the rest of the week and see if we can get you straightened out. Okay?"

I agreed. I didn't have much choice. Obviously Mr. Gellman wasn't going to switch me to another class, and my parents weren't going to let me drop math. Besides, I liked the idea of private lessons with Mr. Farley. Half the girls in the school have crushes on him.

When I got up to leave, Mr. Farley stopped me at the door. "Listen, Marty. I know it's none of my business, but I'm going to give you a piece of advice."

"What?"

"Stay away from Brent Conrad."

"He's a friend of mine."

"He's a troublemaker. He's violent. He drinks too much, and everyone in the school knows he's dealing drugs. You don't need friends like that."

"Thanks for the advice, Mr. Farley. But I think I can choose my own friends. I just need some help with math."

"You seem like a good kid, Marty. I don't want to see you get in trouble. That's all."

I survived the rest of the week. After meeting with Mr. Farley in the morning, I knew exactly what was going on in class, and my hand shot up even faster than Annie's. Besides, Brent didn't come back. He was in school, but he never went to math class. Twice that week he showed up in the cafeteria and talked to me and Rob for a few minutes before he took off with his other friends. That was the only time I saw him. I doubted if he was going to any of his classes. He never carried a notebook or any textbooks. Rob gave him a hard time whenever he saw him.

"You ought to go to your classes, man. You're never going to get out of this place."

"I'm going to English," Brent said.

"Oh, yeah? Must be cute girls in that class, huh?"

Brent winked at him. "And every once in a while I take in a gym class," he added. "Don't want to get too out of shape."

"What about math? You already failed that once."

"I can't stand to see Farley's face. I can't believe I got him again."

I wasn't going to say anything this time, but Brent said it for me. "Marty likes him."

"Everybody likes him," I said. "He's cool."

"He's a jerk. Don't fool yourself, baby."

"What's wrong with him?" I asked Rob after Brent left.

"I told you. Brent hates school. I don't blame him in a way. He's got this reputation. So all the teachers come down hard on him even when he hasn't done anything."

"I don't know why you always have to defend him," I said. "If you ask me, he brings it on himself. Like, what's he got against Farley? Farley's totally cool."

"Last year Farley tried to get Brent kicked out of school."

"What for?"

"He said Brent was dealing drugs. But he couldn't prove it, so Brent got to stay. Farley's got it in for him, though. Keeps trying to catch him at something."

"So," I said, "*is* Brent dealing drugs?"

"No."

"How do you know?"

"I just know. Brent wouldn't do something like that."

Lunch ended, and I went to math class. Brent was there, sitting in the back row. He caught my eye and motioned with his head to the seat next to him. I looked away and sat in my regular seat. Annie was watching me closely.

Mr. Farley came in and started the class. While we were working on a problem, he went over to where Brent was drawing on the desk. I turned around in my seat to watch.

"This class meets five days a week, Conrad. Did it happen to mention that on your schedule?"

Brent didn't answer. He didn't even look up.

"Why do you bother to come at all? That's what I can't figure out."

"I wanna learn math. I'm gonna need it in my future life," Brent muttered, imitating the voice Mr. Farley used when he came in dressed as a greaser.

Mr. Farley went back to his desk and got a textbook, a piece of paper, and a pencil. He gave them to Brent.

"You want to learn math, Conrad? I'm going to make it easy for you. I even brought you a pencil." He started to walk away, then turned back. "Oh, and Conrad, don't worry about what page we're on. Start at the beginning. Page one. You've got some catching up to do."

Mr. Farley started moving around the room, checking people's work, answering questions. I kept watching Brent. He didn't open the book. Mr. Farley came over to my desk. I hadn't even started the problem.

"What's the matter, Marty? I explained this to you this morning. You understood it then."

"I don't feel well. Can I go to the nurse?"

Mr. Farley wrote me a pass, but I didn't go to the

nurse. I went to the bathroom and leaned against the door of a stall, thinking about Mr. Farley and Brent and what Rob had said. I like Mr. Farley. Everybody knows that he's one of the decent teachers, someone who cares about his students. So, why would he want to get Brent kicked out of school? Unless Brent really is dealing drugs. I don't want to believe he would do that any more than Rob does. But I'm not sure. Lately it seems as if Brent doesn't care about anyone or anything.

The bell rang. I waited till I was sure I wouldn't run into Brent. Then I left the bathroom and went to my next class.

Ticket to Paradise

Every time I turn a corner, I see Brent with his arm around a different girl. If I was one of those girls, I'd be embarrassed, but it doesn't seem to bother them. Or maybe each of them thinks she's the one Brent really cares about. Lots of girls want to be with Brent. I know, because whenever Brent hangs out in the cafeteria with me and Rob, all these girls who never talked to me before come over and say, "Hi, Marty! Do you know what the homework is for Spanish? Aren't those language tapes awful?" Before I even have a chance to answer, they glance over at Brent, and he smiles at them. It makes me sick.

I know I should want Brent to have a girlfriend so I won't have to feel guilty, but when I see him with his arm around one of those fakey-fakey girls, I feel even worse. Once I thought I wanted him and Annie to fall in love. Then maybe Annie would understand how I feel about him and stop hating me. And then Brent and Rob and Annie and I could all be together, and that would be perfect. But I think things like that happen only on TV or in trashy novels. In real life, even if they did go out together, I would hate them both so much that I would never speak to them again.

Yesterday, as Rob and I were leaving school, Brent came by on Jimmy's motorcycle. He stopped to talk to us for a minute. Then his eyes started wandering. The girl he picked out was with a group of her friends, but they all conveniently drifted away when Brent roared over and started talking to her. She was cute. All the girls Brent picks are beautiful. Before long, she got on the motorcycle behind Brent and held him around his waist. As they rode off, her long red hair flew out behind her and whipped around her face when they turned the corner.

"I'm going to grow my hair," I said to Rob.

"I like your hair the way it is." He ran his hand through it.

I slipped my hand into his. "Let's go somewhere," I said.

"Can't. I told Mom I'd come straight home and stay with the little guys. She's got a doctor's appointment."

"Please." I leaned my head on his shoulder.

"Cut it out, Marty. I promised her . . ."

"All right. Never mind." I let go of his hand.

"Marty?"

"What?"

"There's something I wanted to talk to you about."

"Go ahead."

"I was thinking of going out for track. Just to keep in shape. Till baseball season."

"Oh."

"They practice after school."

"I know that. I didn't think they practiced at night."

Rob stared at his shoe. "So, how often do they practice?" I asked finally.

"Every day, I think."

"Well, it's been nice knowing you."

"I can still meet you before school. And during lunch."

"Great."

"I know it's not much . . ."

"No, it's not."

"I haven't decided for sure. I was just thinking about it."

"Well, you let me know."

I got on the subway. I was not in a good mood. It bugged me that all the cards that say "Take One" are for careers. Why can't you send away for a brochure that tells you how to make your life tolerable while you're stuck in high school for four years? The closest I could find was an ad for the botanical gardens that said "Ticket to Paradise." So, I went there and looked at the flowers.

I was surprised how many flowers were left in October. They were pretty, but after a while I got bored, so I went to Grandma's.

"What do you think about gardening, Grandma?"

"Gardening? What should I know about gardening?"

"I think I need a hobby."

"Where are you going to have a garden? You live in an apartment building. Besides, it's the wrong time of year."

"There are indoor plants. I could see how many plants I can grow from things we have in the house—carrots, sweet potatoes, bird feed."

"You could."

"You don't like the idea."

"Don't they have activities at school, Marty? Things you could do with people your age?"

"They're all stupid."

"I see. What happened to your boyfriend?"

"I hardly ever see him anymore."

"Why not?"

"School," I said, as if that explained everything. I flopped down on the couch.

"Grandma?"

"What now?"

"Did you ever notice that all the good books have sad endings?"

"I never thought about it."

"Well, it's true."

"I'll take your word for it."

"Why do you think that is?"

"I don't know. Maybe because that's the way life is. It's only in fairy tales that everyone lives happily ever after."

"I'd like to live happily ever after. Wouldn't you?"

"No, thank you."

"Why not?"

Grandma shook her head. "Boring."

I laughed. "Just like a ticket to paradise," I said.

A Little Respect

When I saw Brent standing at the top of the stairs, I thought he must be waiting for some cute girl to walk by.

"Where are you going?" he asked.

"Math class. You know. Farley. Room three-oh-six."

"That class is boring."

I laughed.

"What's so funny about that?" Brent asked.

"Nothing. It just reminded me of something my grandmother said." I was thinking of room 306 as a fairy castle, with Mr. Farley as the handsome prince. I would be the princess, of course, and Annie would be the wicked stepsister. Who would Brent be?

"Let's cut," Brent said.

"Who?" I looked around.

"You and me. Let's go someplace."

"No. I have to go to class."

"You don't *have* to do anything. Why don't you say you *want* to go to class? Say, 'Sorry, Brent, I'd rather go to a math class than hang out with you. I like Mr. Farley, and I don't like you, so why don't you bug off and leave me alone?' "

"Why would I say that? It's not true."

"No? Well, prove it, then."

The bell rang.

"Don't you understand anything?" I asked. I was afraid I was going to cry.

"Yeah, I understand lots of things." All of a sudden he stopped being mean and grinned at me. "I understand that you are dying to go with me. So, admit it, and let's get out of here. I hate this place."

We ran down the stairs.

"Where are we going?"

"The basement."

"The basement?!" It turns out that under the last set of stairs the custodians store brooms and cleaning supplies. Brent sat down on a five-gallon plastic drum of ammonia. There was no place for me to sit, so I leaned against the wall with the brooms.

"You sure do know how to show a girl a good time."

"Hey, I'll take you anywhere you want to go. Anytime. But I didn't think you'd want to leave school. I know you don't like to get in trouble."

"What happens when the custodians come down here? We don't get in trouble?"

"They never come down. I come here with my friends to smoke, and I've never seen anybody."

"Sounds kind of risky."

"I like to live dangerously."

"You think you're pretty cool, don't you?"

"Not really."

"I don't think it's so cool to flunk out of school."

"I don't do it to be cool, Marty."

"I could help you with math."

"What's the point? Farley'll fail me anyway."

"No, he won't. You're paranoid, you know. He can't fail you if you pass the tests."

"Who cares?"

"You don't want to pass, do you?"

Brent shrugged.

"I want you to."

"You're starting to sound like Rob."

"Worse things could happen."

"Sorry. I didn't mean to put down your boyfriend."

"He's your best friend."

"Yeah. But he's him and I'm me. You don't have to like me, but don't try to make me be like him."

"I do like you."

He looked up at me.

"I miss you, little Martha."

"Looks like you've been busy."

"It doesn't mean anything."

"What do you mean?"

"Those girls. They don't mean anything to me."

"Do you tell them that?"

"Do you miss me?"

"I don't know."

"Yeah, you do. I know you do."

He pulled me down so I was sitting on his lap, facing him. He ran his hands up and down my back.

"Why are you doing this, Brent?"

"Just born bad, I guess."

"Stop it," I said softly.

"I don't like the way Rob treats you."

"What are you talking about?"

"He leaves you alone too much. I don't like to think of you being alone all the time."

"He doesn't do it on purpose."

"What does that mean—'on purpose'? He didn't have to go out for track. For that matter, he could tell his parents he's got a girlfriend, and he's going to be spending a lot of time at her house. He could. But he doesn't."

"I love Rob."

"So do I. What's that got to do with it?"

His hands sneaked under my blouse and ran lightly over my stomach, my breasts, under my arms.

"Are you confused, little Martha? Did someone tell you life was supposed to be simple?"

He clamped his arms around me, then stood up. I wrapped my legs around his waist as he kissed me. My body felt glued to Brent no matter how hard my mind tried to pull away.

"Jesus Christ!" the custodian shouted. "Ain't you kids got no place better to go?"

Brent put me down and turned around to face the

custodian. I tried to hide behind Brent. My face was burning hot.

"That's just it," Brent said. "You hit the nail on the head, man. We ain't got no place to go."

Brent was waiting for me outside room 306 the next day with his math book under his arm. "Let's go to class," he said. As we passed Annie, Brent whispered, "Back row. Be there."

Annie ignored him. I sat down. Brent put his book down next to me and went back to where Annie was sitting.

"You want to know a secret?" he asked her.

"What?"

"Come sit with us. I'll tell you."

"I ain't that hard up."

Brent shrugged. "Whatever you say."

All period Brent asked questions. He raised his hand politely, then asked a question like, "What is the plural of hypotenuse?" Mr. Farley answered all of the questions with an absolutely straight face, determined not to show that it was getting to him.

In the middle of class, Brent passed a note to Annie. He showed it to me before he passed it. It said:

I don't believe in geometry. Do you?

When Annie read the note, she laughed in spite of herself. Mr. Farley came over, took the note from her, read it, nodded thoughtfully, stuck it in his pocket, then went on with class.

As we were leaving, Mr. Farley stood by the door. He pulled the note out of his pocket and handed it to Brent. "I think this belongs to you."

Brent took it. "Thanks."

"I want to ask you something, Conrad."

"What?"

"Is there anything you do believe in?"

"Oh. Is this a philosophy class? Or were you speaking in a religious sense? Because I'd rather not discuss my religious beliefs with you. Separation of church and state, and all that jazz."

"I think I know what your problem is."

"My problem is that I don't see how I can accept all those postulates on blind faith. It's been bothering me, man. I'm losing sleep at night."

"You need to learn a little respect, Conrad. You don't have respect for anything or anyone. Not even yourself."

Brent turned to me. "Let's get out of here."

Mr. Farley followed us into the hall and yelled at Brent, "I'll tell you something, Conrad! I'm going to teach you a little respect! You hear me?"

I turned around and glanced back at Mr. Farley. He was standing in the middle of the hall. He looked strange. Then I realized his hands were empty. I had never seen him without something in his hands—a pencil, a book, a piece of chalk. I almost didn't recognize him.

Geometry

The next day Brent spent the whole math period making up proofs. He'd start with a postulate like, "Assume that infinity is two inches long." Then the rest of the proof followed from that. When he got stuck, he passed them to me, so I could add to them.

I looked at the completed proof.

"You could ace this class, you know?"

"Yeah. I think I'll volunteer to put one of these proofs on the board. Farley would love that."

"Why don't you let me help you with the homework?" I asked.

Brent looked right at me. "You want to help me that bad, baby? Who am I to deny you the pleasure?"

"Fine. I'll meet you after school." Since Rob had joined the track team, I didn't have anything to do after school.

"In the library," I added, so he wouldn't get the wrong idea.

"The library? No way. Sorry, kid. I don't do libraries. I break out in hives when I get near a library."

"Very funny."

"You don't believe me? I'll prove it to you. But I should warn you that the last time I went in a library, I swelled up so bad, they had to take me to the hospital . . . I almost died."

"All right. Where do you want to go?"

"I bet a pepperoni pizza and a large Coke would make math go down easier."

After school the pizza place was noisy and crowded.

"Great place to study," I muttered.

"Yeah." Brent was grinning. "That's the trouble with libraries—too quiet. They make me nervous." He squeezed into the booth on the same side I was sitting on, so he could "see the book better." I explained about different kinds of triangles.

"Okay, I think I get it," Brent said, gulping the last of his Coke. "This one's a right triangle and the other two are wrong triangles. Let's go."

"We have to do the homework." I turned to the page with the problems.

"Oh, yeah. The homework. I forgot." Brent rested his head on his hand, staring at me.

"You're not even trying," I said.

"I'm listening."

"You have to look at the diagrams."

"I like looking at you. It helps me concentrate."

I only meant to glance at him, but my eyes got stuck.

"We ought to do the homework," I said finally.

Brent reached over and closed the book.

"Brent . . ."

"I'll do it later. Promise." He crossed his heart.

"But I want to help you."

He was playing with my fingers.

"What kind of help did you have in mind?"

I burst into tears. It surprised me as much as Brent. He put his arm around me.

"I'm sorry, babe. Do you want me to stop? Just tell me if you do, and I'll leave you alone."

"I did tell you."

"I know. But I thought maybe you changed your mind."

I didn't answer.

"Did you?"

"I better go home."

Brent tilted my face up, so I had to look at him.

"Answer me, Marty. Did you change your mind?"

"I don't know," I whispered. I got up and pushed past him, out of the booth, out of the pizza place.

I headed toward school. I needed to talk to Rob. I was going to wait for him to finish track practice. And then I was going to ask him something. But what was I going to ask him? To quit the team? To take me home with him? To be a different person? What good would it do to talk? I knew what he would say. I turned around and headed in the other direction, toward the subway.

I knew where Rob lived, but I had never been to his house. It was a part of the city with houses, each one with its own yard. Where I lived was mostly apartments. There were brownstones, of course. But they looked sort of like apartments, too, and the steps came right down to the pavement. If you wanted grass, you had to go to the park.

I walked up and down in front of Rob's house a few times before I got up my nerve. Then I went and rang the bell. The woman who answered the door was younger than I expected, and pretty. I thought somebody who baked cookies would be plump and wear an apron and maybe even hair curlers.

"Hello," she said. "What can I do for you?" She probably thought I was selling chocolate bars for some worthy cause.

"I'm a friend of Rob's," I said. "Is he home?"

"No. He's still at school. He should be back soon. Do you want to wait for him?"

I could tell she was looking me over, wondering. I nodded.

She stepped back, and I followed her into the living room. Rob's little brothers were sprawled on the floor, building something out of Lego.

"Matt, Jamie, this is Rob's friend . . ." She turned to me. "I'm sorry. I don't know your name."

"Marty," I said.

"This is Marty."

The two boys looked up for a second.

"Hi."

By the time Rob came home I was sitting in the kitchen with Rob's mother and his two brothers, drinking chocolate milk. Matt and Jamie were telling me every joke they'd ever heard. Rob slammed the door.

"Robbie," his mom called, "We're in the kitchen. You have a visitor."

Rob was smiling when he came through the doorway. Then he saw me.

"Hi," I said.

"Hi."

I waited. I wanted to see what he would do. But Rob turned to stone. He just stared at me. Finally, he turned to his mother.

"I guess you met Marty," he said.

"Yes."

I don't know what I expected. But I knew what I wanted. I wanted him to claim me. I wanted him to say, *Mom, this is Marty. She's my girlfriend. She's my best friend. I love her, no matter what you and Dad say.*

Instead, he said, "Marty's in my English class."

"Yes, she told me. I understand you're working on a report together."

"Yeah," Rob mumbled. He wouldn't look at me.

"You didn't give it to me," I said. "I was going to type it tonight."

"I forgot. Sorry. You didn't have to come all the way over here. I could've typed it."

I shrugged. "It doesn't matter."

"Where do you live, Marty?" Rob's mother asked.

I told her.

"If you want to wait, my husband could give you a ride when he gets home."

I glanced at Rob. He still wasn't looking at me.

"No, that's okay. I like to ride the subway. I'll just get the report and be on my way."

Rob rummaged through his book bag and gave me some papers. Then he walked me to the door. The two boys followed us.

"Tell Mom I'm walking Marty to the subway station," he told them.

As soon as we were outside, Rob's control gave out. "What are you doing here?" he hissed.

I was miserable. "I don't know." It was true. I really didn't know.

"You don't know! Marty, I told you—"

"I know. But I thought if they met me, they might like me and then . . ."

"That's not the point. Of course they'd like you. But they'd still forbid me to see you."

"You don't see me anyway."

"I'm sorry, Marty."

"I thought you loved me."

"I *do* love you."

"Then how come we never see each other?"

"I don't expect you to understand."

"Great," I muttered.

"I just didn't think it would be this hard."

"So, what does that mean?"

"I'm not sure."

We were standing outside the subway station by this time.

"So what's going to happen when you go home?"

"Mom will probably ask me if you're my girlfriend. She usually doesn't beat around the bush about stuff like that."

"And what are you going to tell her?"

"Marty, stop it. You know I can't tell her."

I kicked an empty beer can near my foot. I felt like smashing bottles, the way Brent did. Instead, I said, very quietly, "I guess your parents were right."

"What do you mean?"

"Maybe you're not ready to have a girlfriend."

Rob stared at me for what seemed like a long time.

"Maybe not," he said finally.

And suddenly there was nothing left to say.

Half and Whole

I didn't want to see anyone. Of course, I didn't meet Rob before school, and in English class I found a new place to sit, on the other side of the room.

I kept telling myself that it was stupid to feel bad. Rob and I hardly saw each other anyway, so what difference did it make? But I couldn't help it. I felt as if someone had ripped me in half. I didn't even want to see Brent. I wanted to be alone where no one could see me ripped apart like that.

At lunchtime I stayed in the girls' bathroom as long as I could. I fooled around with my hair and put on red nail polish. Then I went to my locker. Brent was there, leaning against my locker, waiting for me.

He didn't seem to notice that I was ripped in half. Or

maybe he always knew it. Maybe he knew all along that I couldn't really be connected to Rob the way I wanted to be. The truth is, I didn't care what he knew or didn't know. He was waiting for me, and it seemed as if that was all that mattered.

"Come outside with me," he said.

I followed him down the hall. He didn't look back to see if I was coming, but when we got outside, he turned to face me. There was no one around. He was standing really close, but he wasn't touching me. There was a little space between us. Nothing like the space I sometimes felt between me and Rob. The space didn't matter because I felt him reaching out to me, wanting me, wanting me to want him.

"Yes," I said.

A little smile started to twitch at the corners of his mouth.

"Yes?"

"Yes, I changed my mind."

Brent grinned a great big, happy, simple grin. Then he kissed me. And if my mouth hadn't been so busy kissing, I would have been grinning, too.

When we stopped kissing, Brent held me really close to him and whispered, "Let's get out of here."

Brent was still holding me as we started walking. I was walking backward, but I wasn't scared. I knew Brent wouldn't let me fall. He started kissing me again as we walked. I knew I should have been embarrassed, but there was no one around. And besides, I didn't care.

"Hey!" The voice came from behind us, over near the

entrance to the school. "What are you doing out here? Where do you think you are going?"

Brent let go of me.

"Come on, Marty. Run!"

But I looked back. It was Mr. Farley. The prince from the fairy castle, and he broke the spell. I stopped.

Mr. Farley walked over to us. "Well, if it isn't Mr. Conrad," he said. "I should have known. But you, Marty, I'm disappointed in you. I thought you had more sense."

I didn't say anything. There was no point in antagonizing him. We were already in enough trouble.

"I'll tell you what," Mr. Farley continued. "I'm going to give you a break because I don't really think you're a bad kid, Marty. If you just go on inside and don't give me any trouble, I'm going to forget all about this. Fair enough?"

I nodded and started to walk back to the building. It wasn't till I opened the door and held it open for Brent that I realized he hadn't followed me. I turned around. He was still standing exactly where I left him, staring at Mr. Farley.

"Don't be stupid, Conrad. Get inside before I change my mind."

"Don't do me any favors, Farley."

"Okay. If that's the way you want it. Nothing would give me more pleasure than to give you detention. Except maybe having you suspended. Or expelled. Let's see what we can do about that, huh, Conrad? What have you got in your pockets?"

"None of your damn business," Brent told him.

145

I was still watching as Mr. Farley grabbed the front of Brent's jacket with one hand and started slapping him lightly with the other as if he were frisking him.

"Where do you keep your drugs, Conrad? Up here, close to your heart?" Mr. Farley slapped Brent's chest. "Or down here? Close to your balls?"

Brent pulled away as Mr. Farley lowered his hand.

"Keep your hands off me!" he shouted. Then he turned and ran down the street. Mr. Farley hesitated for only a second before he ran after him.

I watched from the doorway, paralyzed, not knowing what to do. Finally, when they disappeared around a corner, I started after them. I caught up with them in an alley. I never would have found them, except that I heard Mr. Farley shouting. He had cornered Brent. The alley dead-ended, and there was no way out. Brent had his back against the wall of a building, and Mr. Farley was screaming at him.

"You lousy, no-good punk! You think you're hot stuff, don't you? But you're nothing! You're a worm! You're a maggot! You feed off of other people. It makes me sick to see you with a decent girl like Marty. I ought to teach you a lesson, Conrad. I ought to take you and knock some sense into you. I ought to—"

Mr. Farley was moving toward Brent. I was scared. I didn't know what he was going to do. Neither of them had noticed me. I rushed at Mr. Farley.

"Leave him alone!" I said. "He isn't hurting anybody! Why don't you leave him alone?"

Mr. Farley turned to face me. I had that feeling

again—that I didn't recognize him. His face was red and angry, and his hands were clenched into fists. He took a deep breath, and when he spoke it was cold and hard. And very quiet. Too quiet.

"Go back to school, Marty," he said. "This has nothing to do with you."

"I'm not leaving without Brent," I said. I turned to Brent. His face was all twisted up.

"Get out of here, Marty," he said. "I'll be okay. I'll call you later."

I hesitated. I didn't see how I could leave, but I knew it was making it harder for Brent, knowing I was there, watching.

"Marty." Brent was reaching toward me again, across the space between us. "Please, go."

I turned and walked away, slowly at first. Then I started to run. I was crying and running, and I ran all the way back to school. But I couldn't go in. I had to know that Brent was all right. I had to go back and see that he was all right.

When I got back to the entrance of the alley, I could see a cluster of people at the end. I couldn't see Brent or Mr. Farley. I ran down the alley and pushed through the people standing there. Brent was lying on the ground, unconscious. I ran over to him. He looked awful. His head was bleeding and his face was bruised. I started to cry again. I tried to put my arms around him, but I didn't want to hurt him any more, and I didn't know what other parts of him were crushed or broken. I turned to the people standing around him.

147

"What happened?" I demanded.

"Don't really know," one man said. "I heard shouting and thuds, like a fight or something, so I ran out here. But by the time I got here, the kid was lying on the ground. There was another guy. Older guy. Said he was going to call an ambulance."

"Didn't anyone see what happened?" I asked. The rest shook their heads. I felt like some wild animal protecting my own. I thought I would kill anyone who tried to come near Brent.

Maybe the people standing around understood how I felt, because they wandered off and I was alone with Brent in the alley. I leaned over and kissed the bruised places on his face very, very gently.

"You'll be all right," I whispered. "I'll stay with you. And you'll be all right."

Then I leaned my head on his chest. I could feel his heart beating, so I knew he was alive. I closed my eyes and listened to his heart and felt as if there were nothing else in the world but us.

That's how Mr. Farley found us when he came back. I didn't even hear him coming till he put his hand on my shoulder and said "Marty."

I jumped up.

"There's an ambulance coming. They'll be here in a few minutes."

I guess I was staring at him. I didn't even ask him what had happened. Mr. Farley leaned toward Brent.

"Stay away from him," I said.

"Marty, I know what you must be thinking, but that's not the way it was. After you left, Brent went crazy. He lost control. He started throwing himself against the wall. Over and over. I tried to stop him. But he was thrashing and kicking, and I couldn't get anywhere near him."

I was still standing between him and Brent. I didn't say anything.

"I know I was angry. But I would never, ever hurt a student. I hope you believe that."

"I don't know," I whispered.

"Marty, Brent uses drugs. Maybe you don't want to accept that. But he does. He's probably on something now. And drugs will make people do terrible things. Crazy things." Mr. Farley looked past me at Brent. "Wasted," he said. "That's what they say, isn't it? When someone's on drugs—that he's 'wasted'? It's a terrible, terrible thing to waste a life."

Mr. Farley put his hand on my arm. His hand was shaking.

"I'm sorry about Brent, Marty. I'm sorry I get so angry. I just can't stand to see someone waste his life. And I can't stand by and watch him drag you down with him."

I didn't have a chance to answer him because the ambulance arrived. Mr. Farley talked to the driver while they put Brent on a stretcher. Then he came back to me.

"I have to go back to school. I need to notify Brent's parents. They'll take over from here. I want you to come back to school with me."

"I'm going with Brent," I said.

"Don't be foolish, Marty. There's nothing you can do."

"I want to go with Brent," I said again.

Mr. Farley held up his hands in a helpless gesture. I stared at them, remembering the day he stood in the hallway with his hands empty and his face red, shouting at Brent that he was going to teach him respect. Could he use those same empty hands to beat Brent's head against a wall? Did he think he could beat a little respect into Brent?

At the hospital they made me sit in the waiting room until Brent was all bandaged up. His parents still hadn't arrived, so the nurses let me sit in his room next to his bed as long as I promised to be quiet.

When Brent finally opened his eyes, he tried to sit up, but it hurt too much.

"What the hell—" He looked around, saw me, and tried to smile. "Hey," he said.

"Hey, to you."

"Come over here."

I sat on the bed next to him.

"Does it hurt?" I asked.

"Yeah, it hurts."

"Do you remember what happened?" It obviously hurt him to talk. But he started, pausing often between words. "Farley," he said. "The guy went nuts. Grabbed me. Threw me against the wall. Never knew the bastard was so strong."

The nurse came in. "Your friend needs to rest," she said. "You can come back tomorrow."

"She's not bothering me," Brent said.

"She's really not supposed to be here. But I didn't see any harm in her sitting by the bed till you woke up. Now she'll have to go."

"Can I just say good-bye?" Brent asked the nurse. "Like in private?"

The nurse left the room.

"Come closer," Brent said. I leaned over toward him. "Closer." I rested my head on his chest again, the way I had in the alley, and Brent reached up and touched my hair. "Marty," he said, "I love you."

Believing

The next day I skipped school and went straight to the hospital. It wasn't visiting hours, and I knew they'd kick me out, but I wanted to sneak in and see Brent, at least for a minute.

Brent was awake. His head was still bandaged, but he looked a lot better. I stood in the doorway till he noticed me. Then we were looking at each other. Neither of us seemed to know what to say. Something had happened between us. But I didn't know what it was or what it meant. All of a sudden I felt shy.

"Aren't you supposed to be in school?" Brent asked.

"Yes, but—"

"Am I a bad influence on you, little Martha?"

I didn't answer.

"That's what Farley kept saying. He kept telling me to leave you alone."

"I heard him," I mumbled.

"Maybe he's right."

"Don't say that."

"I'm not as bad as Farley thinks."

"You're not bad," I said.

Brent looked at me.

"Do you believe everything Farley says about me?" he asked.

"No."

"Why not?"

I shrugged. "I don't understand why Farley hates you so much."

"He thinks I'm evil. He thinks I snare innocent children and force them into a life of drugs, crime, and prostitution. If the guy is such a crusader, I don't know why he doesn't go after the Mafia and leave me alone."

"*Do* you sell drugs?" I asked.

"Is this a test?"

I realized I was still standing in the doorway. I walked in and stood by his bed.

"No. I just want to know."

"Yeah, sometimes—if I've got the stuff and someone comes looking for it."

I traced the folds of the sheet with my finger. I didn't know what to say.

"Marty," Brent said, "I didn't cause the problem. I didn't make kids feel so bad that they've got to get stoned every morning so they can get through the day."

153

"Is that how you feel?"

"Sometimes."

"It's not much of a solution."

"No."

"Did you throw yourself against that wall yesterday?"

"Is that what Farley told you?"

I nodded.

"I figured. That's what he told my parents, too. I told them he was lying to cover his ass, but they didn't believe me. You probably don't believe me, either."

Before I could answer, the nurse came in and told me I had to leave. As I turned to go, Brent asked me if I would go to his house and bring him a notebook with some of his drawings.

"There's something I want you to see," he said.

Even though Brent gave me the key, I felt as if I was breaking into his house. It was the middle of the day, and I knew his parents wouldn't be home. Still, I was careful not to make a sound. Brent's house looked like something in a magazine. No clutter. No mess. It didn't look like anyone lived there.

I peeked into the dining room. A crystal bowl full of fruit was set in the middle of a carved wooden table. I tried to imagine Brent sitting with his parents at dinner. Brent's parents would talk to each other about work and world politics, turning to Brent only to say "Pass the peas, son."

It wasn't so easy to find the notebook in Brent's room. There were clothes and records and comics all over the floor and the bed. Obviously, Brent's parents never set foot in this room. The notebook wasn't on the shelf where he told me it would be. I rummaged around and finally found it under his pillow. It seemed like something a young child would do—keeping something safe under his pillow. Like a lost tooth waiting for the tooth fairy.

I spent the rest of the morning riding the subway, trying not to look at the drawings. I was dying to see them, but it didn't seem right to look at something so private without permission. Instead, I thought about Mr. Farley. I didn't want to believe that he could have actually slammed Brent against the wall. But I didn't want to believe that Brent did it to himself, either. I didn't want to believe that even more.

"Did you look at them?" Brent asked as soon as I handed him the notebook.

"No, I—"

"Here." Brent handed the notebook back to me. "Go ahead."

I opened the book and started to look through it. The first half was filled with comics. The drawings were good, but I didn't really look closely. I'm not that interested in space invaders or super heroes. I glanced at Brent, wondering why he wanted me to see this.

"Keep going," Brent said.

The middle of the notebook was empty. Blank pages. I flipped to the back. The last few pages were different. There were several drawings in black and white. Brent's impressions of life in the city. Women in fur coats walking poodles past bag ladies, skyscrapers towering over slums and a limousine running over the body of an addict with a needle stuck in his arm. Another drawing showed men and women in business suits, each one wearing a Walkman, marching single file along a course marked off with little flags. The caption at the bottom read: "Marching to the Beat of the Same Drummer."

I didn't look up from the drawings, but I knew Brent was watching me. I turned to the last page. It was the only drawing in color. Bright Magic Marker colors. Everything Brent and I had done together was in that picture: the Cyclone, the ferry, the motorcycle-roller-skate ride, and Brent's arms around me as we swung the bat in the park.

I looked up.

"Do you like it?" Brent asked.

I nodded.

"Lie down next to me," Brent said.

I was afraid Brent's parents would walk in, but he insisted there was no chance that they would show up till after dinner.

"Aside from about five hundred nurses, doctors, orderlies, aides, kitchen staff, and cleaning people, we're completely alone," he assured me.

"Marty," Brent whispered when I was snuggled up close to him, "let's run away."

I laughed. "We're too young," I said.

"I look a lot older. I could get a job someplace. I could take care of you."

I didn't say anything. I couldn't tell if he was serious.

"Will you think about it?"

"Okay, I'll think about it."

"Lots of teen-agers run away, and their parents never find them."

I was getting scared that he really meant it.

"Let's not talk anymore, okay?"

"Okay," he said, and kissed me.

I was lying next to Brent, but I couldn't relax. I kept thinking about him wanting to run away. If anyone else had said it, I'd know they would never have the guts to do it. But with Brent I wasn't too sure.

It must have been because I was on edge that I sensed someone was coming. I jumped off the bed.

"What's wrong?" Brent asked.

At that moment Rob walked in.

"Hey, Robbie!" Brent said. "How'd you know I was here?"

"Your parents called me last night," Rob answered Brent, but he was staring at me.

"Hi," I said. I didn't know what else to do. I knew there wasn't much chance of the earth opening up and swallowing me. And Rob kept staring at me.

"So, what did my parents say?" Brent tried to break the tension. "Did they want you to get me to confess my sins?"

"I just wanted to see how you were," Rob muttered.

"But I guess I came at a bad time. I'll come back later."

"No," I said. "You stay. I've got to get home anyway."
I started for the door.

"Marty?" I stopped, but I didn't turn around to look at Brent. "I'll call you later, okay?"

"Okay," I said, then left the room. I thought all I wanted was to get out of there, out of that room, out of the hospital, out into the crowded, noisy streets, where I could breathe. But once I was in the hall, I stopped. I glanced back into the room. Rob was staring at the foot of the bed, where the notebook was lying open. I could even see the bright, flashy colors from where I was standing.

"What's happening at school?" Brent asked.

"Lots of rumors. Everybody's talking about you and Farley."

"I'm famous, huh?"

"Farley wasn't in school today. Somebody told me there's going to be some kind of investigation. Farley could be in a lot of trouble."

"Oh, sure. It's his word against mine. I wonder who they're going to believe. Nobody else was there."

"Nobody?" Rob glanced back at the drawing.

"Hey, Robbie, I don't blame you for being pissed off. I—"

"Why didn't you tell me?"

"I didn't want to hurt you, man. It just happened. Sometimes things happen . . ."

"Look, forget it, okay? It doesn't matter. Just forget about it."

158

"She loves you, Rob."

Rob didn't answer. Maybe he nodded. Maybe he stared at his shoe. Maybe he cried, like me.

I wanted to be in bed when Mom got home so I could tell her I was sick and didn't go to school. It's hard to fool Mom about being sick since she's a nurse, but I told her I had diarrhea and was throwing up all day. I don't think I looked too good, so maybe she believed me.

Brent didn't call. I figured his parents were probably visiting him. I thought about calling Rob. But I couldn't imagine what I would say to him. I even started thinking that running away wasn't such a bad idea after all.

Since I was sick, I didn't get to eat supper, but I didn't have much appetite anyway. Mom brought me tea and dry toast, and Dad went out to the store to get ginger ale. I told them I was feeling better, which was the biggest lie of all.

I lay in bed, but I couldn't sleep. I kept thinking about what it would be like to leave home forever and never come back. And every time I decided that I couldn't do that, I thought about never seeing Brent again. And I knew I couldn't do that, either.

When the phone rang, I picked it up on the first ring. Brent started sobbing right away. "Marty? You've got to help me!"

"Brent! What's wrong? What happened?"

"My parents were here. They didn't even go to work today. They spent the whole day talking to school psychologists and guidance counselors and shrinks, and they came to the conclusion that they should put me in a mental hospital because I'm a danger to myself and maybe to others, too." All that came out in a rush, full of anger. Then his voice got tiny. "What am I going to do?"

"They can't do that," I said. "How can they do that?"

"You don't understand. I'm a minor. They own me. Until I turn eighteen they can do whatever they want with me."

"We have to convince them that Farley's lying. Maybe I can talk to them. I'll tell them about seeing Farley yelling at you."

"It wouldn't help. Farley admits he was yelling at me. He says he feels terrible about it, like he might be partly responsible for what happened. Besides, even if you'd seen him slam my head against the wall, my parents wouldn't believe you because you're a friend of mine."

"There's got to be something we can do. I'll come see you tomorrow. We'll talk about it some more. We'll figure something out."

"Marty?"

"What?"

"Don't hang up, okay? I just need to know you're there. Please, don't hang up."

"Okay," I said. "I'm here. It's all right. I'm still here."

Escape

The next day was Saturday, so I didn't have to go to school. But I couldn't convince my parents that I was well enough to go out. Mom said I should stay home and rest, even though I was feeling better, so I wouldn't get sick again.

I tried to call Brent to tell him why I couldn't come, but a nurse answered and said he couldn't talk on the phone. I got scared that they'd already taken him away to the mental hospital, and no one would tell me where he was, and I'd never see him again. Mom would probably say that things like that happen only in soap operas and trashy novels, but I'm not too sure, so I had to get over to the hospital to find out.

I waited till Mom and Dad went out to do the week's grocery shopping. Then I left the apartment. The hospital was a long walk from the subway station, and it was hot. "Unseasonably warm," they would say on the news. Much too warm for the clothes I had put on. I was sweating by the time I reached the hospital. Inside it was cool. They must have put on the air-conditioning. The sweat under my arms turned cold.

Brent's room was empty. I went out into the corridor.

"Where is he?" I demanded as soon as I saw the nurse who had kicked me out the day before.

"Where is who?"

"Brent. Brent Conrad. He was in this room. And now he's gone. Did you transfer him to another room?"

"Are you family?"

"No."

"I'm afraid I can't—"

"I'm his friend. I have to know where he is. You have to tell me where he is!" I knew that getting hysterical wasn't going to convince her, but I couldn't help it.

The nurse started to walk away. I followed her. "Please help me. I just want to know where he is," I told her a little more calmly.

"He's left the hospital," she said. "That's all I can tell you. I suggest you call his family." Then she stepped into a patient's room and closed the door.

I sat on the steps in front of the hospital, trying to think. *Let's run away,* he had said. *Let's run away.* I kept hearing him say it over and over in my mind. Would he take off without me? Without even telling me? Without saying good-bye? It didn't make any sense.

162

I got back on the subway. When I'd left the apartment, I thought maybe I would get back before my parents got home. But I couldn't go home without finding out where Brent was.

I went first to the abandoned building. There were a few guys there drinking beer. No one had seen Brent. I wandered through the building, looking in every room. He wasn't anywhere. I sat down on the tattered mattress on the third floor where we used to sit and talk during the summer, and I started to cry. I had no idea where he could be. I was sure he must have plenty of places around the city that he used to hide, but I had no way to know where they were. Rob might know something, but I didn't dare call him.

I went back out to the street and called home. Mom was furious that I'd sneaked out while she and Dad were gone. I told her I was really sorry, but I couldn't stand to be cooped up anymore, and it was such a nice, warm day. . . . She wanted to know where I was, of course. I told her I was with Annie. That softened her up. Sometimes I think she feels even worse than I do about me and Annie not being friends anymore.

"Oh," she said. "Well, give her my love."

"Okay, Mom." I tried to sound offhand. "Did anyone call me?"

"No. Why?"

"Nothing. I just wondered."

"When are you coming home?"

"Well, I was thinking . . . I mean, I know you're mad

at me and everything, but I wanted to know if I could stay over at Annie's."

"Marty, you've been sick, and if you stay at Annie's you'll be up late. I don't think it's a good idea."

"I feel fine. Besides, tomorrow's Sunday. I can sleep late. Please, Mom. I haven't seen Annie in such a long time." I knew that would get her.

"Oh, all right."

"Thanks, Mom."

I hung up, feeling worse than ever. I still didn't know where Brent was, and now I couldn't even go home. I should have just gone home and waited for him to call. He was bound to call me eventually.

I rode the subway to McDonald's. The one where Annie works. Now that I'd told my mother I was with her, I had to get her to cover for me. I had no reason to hope that she would. But I thought maybe, if she knew I had a problem, a really bad problem, maybe she'd forget that she hated me. Maybe she'd even want to help.

I stood in line and waited my turn. When she got to me, she said, "May I help you?" She had this crooked little smile on her face, as if she thought she was being funny.

"Annie, I need to talk to you."

"It's kind of busy. Saturday and all."

"Don't you get a break?"

She glanced at the clock behind her.

"Half an hour."

"I'll wait."

"Suit yourself," she said.

I ordered a Coke and sat in one of the booths. I blew bubbles in the Coke with my straw and read the menu over and over. It doesn't take much to memorize the menu at McDonald's.

Annie finally slipped into the booth opposite me. "What's up?"

"I'm worried about Brent," I said.

"You come all the way over here and wait half an hour to tell me that?"

I told her everything that had happened. I knew her break wouldn't be very long, so I talked fast and left out a lot of things, but she got the idea.

"Annie," I said finally, "do you think his parents could've put him in a mental hospital already?"

Annie shook her head. "I doubt it. It takes time to arrange those things. I bet he just took off someplace."

I started to cry. "Why wouldn't he tell me?"

"Oh, Marty. Maybe it's just as well. That boy is nothing but trouble."

"I have to find him."

"What do you see in him, anyway?"

Annie sounded annoyed. I wanted her to understand. I knew I could never explain it to Rob, but maybe I could make Annie understand.

"I know you think Rob's a great guy," I said. "I do, too. I really do. But he's all wrapped up like a package, smooth and neat. It's pretty, and I want it, and I can hold it in my hands, but I'm not allowed to open it."

I was afraid to look at her, afraid to see on her face that she thought I was nuts and had no idea what I was talking about. So, I just kept going.

"Every time I'm with Brent, I feel like he tears himself open and pulls out a little piece of himself and gives it to me to keep." I stopped. I still didn't want to look at Annie.

"That ain't love, Marty. That's some kind of sick. The boy needs help."

"Then I'll help him."

"You can't do it by yourself."

"I can try. Maybe I can."

"Marty," Annie said sharply. I finally looked up at her. "You got to let him go."

"What am I supposed to do with all those little pieces of him?" I asked miserably.

Annie stood up. "I got to go back to work. What did you expect me to do anyway? Help you look for him?"

I'd almost forgotten why I came.

"I told my mom I was staying at your house tonight."

"Great," Annie muttered. "Feel free to invite yourself over anytime."

"Annie, if I find him, would you cover for me, in case my mother calls?"

Annie hesitated. Her manager caught sight of her.

"Let's move it, Anna!" he yelled. "We've got a busy Saturday situation here. Let's go!"

"Annie, please. This is really important to me."

"All right." Annie spoke quietly. I barely heard her. She started to walk away before I could even say thank you. Then suddenly she turned back and looked down at me. "You ain't pregnant, are you?"

"No! We haven't done anything."

Annie kept staring at me, looking me up and down, inside out and every which way. She knew me better than anybody else did.

"Maybe not," she said finally. "But you will." Suddenly she grabbed both my hands and squeezed them tight in hers. "You be careful," she said, before she turned again and ran back to her station.

I walked back outside and stood on the street in front of McDonald's. I didn't know what to do next. Then it hit me. The shed. If Brent was Rob's best friend, he must know about the shed. And he would want me to find him. He would hide someplace where I would find him.

Brent was asleep. It was a long time before he even stirred. I didn't mind. I was so happy to see him, I could have stayed there forever, watching him. I tried not to think about what was going to happen next.

When he did wake up, Brent acted as if he knew I would be there. He turned over on his back and stretched.

"What time is it?" he asked.

"It must be about five o'clock."

"What took you so long?" He winked at me.

"Why didn't you call me? Why didn't you tell me where you were?"

"I knew you'd find me."

"Or Rob would." The words just came out of my mouth. But as soon as I said them, I knew it was true. If Rob was looking for Brent, this would be the first place he would look. It wasn't me that Brent was waiting for. It was Rob.

"What's that supposed to mean?" Brent asked me.

"Has Rob been here?"

That's when I noticed the sleeping bag. And the remains of a pizza and Cokes.

"Yeah, he was here. He brought me some stuff."

"Is he coming back?" I was ready to scramble out of the shed as fast as I could. I thought for sure I would die if Rob found me there.

"No. You know his family. He had to get home. He said he'd come back in the morning."

I relaxed a little. But I still didn't want to be there. In fact, I would rather have been almost anywhere else at that moment.

"Well, I guess you don't need anything," I said. I didn't even know if I could get out through the hole in the roof by myself. Rob had always helped me.

"Marty, Rob's my best friend."

"I know." I was starting to cry. I felt as if I was losing everything. I wondered if Annie would let me stay if I went to her house. "Rob would do anything for you," I added.

"What about you?"

Brent was leaning against the wall of the shed. His fingers were picking off splinters of wood. I stood in the middle of the shed. My hands were empty. I wished I had something to pick at with my fingers.

Brent was watching me. "Marty, I can't go to that hospital. You know what they do to you in those places? If you're not crazy when you go in, you are by the time they get through with you."

"What are you planning to do?"

"I told you. I'm going to run away."

"Did you tell Rob that?"

"No."

"What does he think you should do?"

"He wants to talk to my parents, try to change their minds. But I know it's no use."

"It's worth a try."

"You don't know them. They've never given me a chance. Why should they start now?"

I didn't know what to say. Brent was still picking bits of wood off the wall.

"Will you come with me?" he asked.

I couldn't answer him. I couldn't say yes and I couldn't say no. Either possibility was unbearable.

"Is it because of Rob?" he asked.

I shook my head.

"Do you love him?"

"I don't know," I whispered.

Brent slipped down the side of the shed till he was

sitting on the ground, hunched over, hugging his knees. I reached out to touch him. "I love *you*," I said.

Brent jumped up. "Prove it!" he shouted at me. Then he grabbed me and kissed me hard, his tongue pushing inside my mouth, his body pressing against mine, pushing me back against the wall of the shed. I couldn't move.

It wasn't until he tried to take my clothes off that I started to fight. I pushed him away as hard as I could. I caught him off guard, and he stumbled backward. Then he came back at me, and we fought. I was scratching and kicking and hitting. I didn't care if he was still recovering from getting his head bashed. I hated him.

Brent's strength wore out quickly. He should still have been in the hospital. He sat on the hard dirt floor of the shed and started to shake. I was shaking, too, but it was nothing like Brent. Brent's whole body heaved with each breath. It was something like crying, but no sound came out. I watched him, imagining the crying trapped inside like a wild animal rattling its cage till the whole thing shook.

When he spoke, it was a tiny sound, like that same trapped animal calling for help.

"I'm scared, Marty," he said. "I don't know what to do."

I knelt in front of him and put my finger on his lips. "Don't talk anymore," I said. I didn't know what to do, either. I just knew that I wanted to give him something, whatever he needed. All of me. I started to pull off my clothes. But Brent closed his hands around mine.

"Don't," he said.

Then he put his arms around me and held me.

I tried to stay awake all night, so I could feel Brent's arms around me and hear him breathing. But I must have fallen asleep just before dawn. And when I woke up, he was gone.

Like in the Movies

I'm not sure exactly when it hit me that Brent wasn't
ever coming back. At first I didn't believe that somebody
could disappear like that. I thought the police would
find him and bring him home. I didn't know whether
to hope they would or not. My whole body missed him,
and all the rest of me, too. But I knew if they found
him, we'd be right back where we started.

Most of all, I wanted him to come and find me, like
in the movies. I'd come home one day and, as I got near
my building, I'd hear someone call me from the alley-
way.

Martha.

It would be a hoarse whisper, and when I heard it, a
shiver would run through my body. I'd stop for a mo-

ment at the entrance to the alley. It would be dark, and I wouldn't see him at first.

Brent?

I'd start to turn away, thinking I'd imagined it. Then he'd step out from a doorway, and I'd stop breathing, tears springing into my eyes as we ran to each other. I'd touch him all over to be sure he was real, and then he would kiss me.

That's about as far as that fantasy ever went, because after that I knew he'd ask me to go back with him. That would be the reason he came. And as much as I was dying to see him and hold him, I still knew I couldn't go. Not even in my imagination.

Anyway, scenes like that happen only in the movies, not in real life. So, he never came or called or even sent a postcard. I read an article in the newspaper about teenage runaways. Most of them become prostitutes or street hustlers or drug dealers and are out there on their own for years. Maybe that's when it hit me. They weren't going to find him. They weren't going to bring him back. And I was never going to see him again.

Alive

Rob had God to get him through this. I envied him. I wished I could talk to God. Every day I came home from school and lay on my bed and stared at the ceiling. I didn't even feel like riding the subway.

Annie and Grandma tried to cheer me up. And Mom and Dad worried about me. But it didn't help. Rob was the only person who might have understood. But, of course, I couldn't talk to him.

I was way behind in all my classes. I never did any homework, and I couldn't concentrate in class. I stopped going to math class altogether.

Eventually, Mr. Farley called my parents. I don't know what took him so long, but maybe he wasn't too eager to see me, either. He was the third teacher to call home that week. After Dad talked to Mr. Farley, he came into my room.

"That was your math teacher," Dad said.

I didn't look up from the magazine I was reading.

"He says you haven't been in class for three weeks."

"That's true."

"Why not?"

"I tried to tell you the first week of school that I wanted to drop math. You said I could handle it, but you were wrong, Dad. I gave it a chance, and I can't handle it."

"You know that's not the problem, Martini."

"What did Mr. Farley say the problem was?"

"He said you'd gotten mixed up with some trouble-makers."

"Give me a break."

"Mr. Farley wants to have a conference with you and me and Mom."

"Do we have to? Couldn't I just drop math?"

"You could. But it's not a great way to deal with problems."

I was leaning against the headboard with my arms crossed, each hand clutching the opposite arm. I wished that Dad would put his arms around me and hold me tight. *It hurts, Daddy,* I said inside my head. *Can you make it stop? It hurts so bad.*

Dad got up and went to the door.

"Mr. Farley said he would call back tomorrow. Think

about it. We'll discuss it when I get home from work. Okay?"

Mom and Dad both had to take off from work to meet with Mr. Farley. He explained to them everything that had happened, even giving Brent's version of the story. He seemed so fair and thoughtful, and especially concerned about me, how could anyone doubt his sincerity? Finally he turned to me.

"What do you say, Marty? Can we give it another chance?"

I had been staring out the window while he talked to my parents. I didn't turn around.

"I don't think I can handle math right now," I said softly. "I tried to tell my parents and Mr. Gellman and you from the start."

"I know you can do it when you put your mind to it. You were doing very well for a while."

I didn't answer.

"Look, Marty," Mr. Farley continued, "I'm not trying to prove anything to you or to myself. If you don't want to be in my class, that's fine. We'll find another math class for you. I don't want you to give up on math because of this. That's what worries me most—it's the effect Brent has had on you. He's a destructive person. He didn't only have a problem with me. He hated school, he hated authority of any kind, he had no respect for anyone or anything. I don't want to see you turn out like that. I told you that at the beginning of the year."

"You don't know anything about him." I was starting to cry.

"He's a very disturbed young man, Marty. I understand you care about him, and I admire your loyalty, but you have to think about yourself, about your future. Don't mess up your life because of this."

Mr. Farley turned back to my parents.

"I've spoken with some of Marty's other teachers. She's failing all of her courses. I think there is real cause for concern."

I stood up. "I want to drop math," I said.

"Marty," Mom said, "I know you're way behind, but maybe you could get help after school. Is that possible?" she asked Mr. Farley.

He nodded. "If she wants to, we could work something out."

"I don't want to."

"You have to do something, Marty. We're not going to sit here and let you fail all of your courses. What *do* you think we should do about it?"

"Nothing," I said.

"Marty—" Mom's voice was starting to rise.

I finally looked at them. I looked from one face to the other. Inside me a tiny, vicious creature was scrambling around, scratching and kicking and biting. My stomach, my heart, my lungs, all my insides were torn and bleeding. It hurt like hell.

"I want to drop math," I said again, then ran out into the hall.

Classes had just gotten out, which was bad luck because tears were streaming down my face, and everybody was staring at me. I started down the stairs and saw Rob coming up toward me. I turned around and ran back up and took another staircase. I'm not sure, but I thought maybe I heard Rob call my name.

I didn't know what to do. I wanted to go into the girls' bathroom and wash my face and blow my nose and go to my next class. I'm sure that's what most people would have done. But I couldn't do it. I could hardly breathe with that little creature clutching at me inside. I was scared. I even thought maybe I should go to the hospital. I got this idea in my head that I was dying. Maybe that was what was wrong with me, why I lay on my bed all the time. It wasn't that I was weird or sad or a psychological wreck. I was just dying.

I pushed through all the people standing near the entrance to the school. The teacher on duty saw me leave the building. He started toward me, and I ran. I thought of Brent running from Mr. Farley, and for a second I wondered if this guy would chase me. He didn't. He only yelled after me, "Hey! You know you're not allowed to leave school! Get back here! What's your name?"

I kept running. The air was cold, and it was easier to breathe, so I gave up the idea of going to the hospital. I ran and ran and ran. I wasn't surprised to find myself in the park. Hardly anyone was around. It was a cold, nasty day. Anyone with any sense was inside.

I hadn't been in the shed since Brent disappeared. I leaned against the wall. My heart was pounding like crazy. I closed my eyes and tried to slow down my breathing. The way my breath came out, gasping, it sounded almost like sobbing.

I don't remember what happened after that. I know I fell asleep eventually. I dreamed Rob was with me, lying next to me, touching my face with his fingertips. Only it wasn't a dream. I opened my eyes, and he was there, really, beside me.

"I thought I'd find you here," he said. "I saw you at school. When you caught a glimpse of me and turned around and ran the other way, something snapped in me. I thought, *we can't let this happen to us.* It probably sounds crazy, but Brent was there, too. He was standing next to me, and he put his arm around my shoulder, and he said, 'Don't let her get away, Robbie. Don't let them win.' I don't know if that makes any sense to you."

He stopped to look at me. I nodded, and he went on. "You see, it was the first time . . ." Rob trailed off.

"What?" I asked.

"It was the first time since Brent left that I felt . . ."

I wasn't sure if he was ever going to finish that sentence. "You felt what?" I really wanted to know.

The last word came out as a whisper, but I heard him. "Alive," he said.

In Real Life

After Rob went home, I got on the subway. A group of black guys with a huge boom box got on at the next stop. They made me think of that girl I saw dancing in the park. I wished I could talk to her. I wanted to ask her what ever happened with that boy she liked. I wanted to tell her that I finally got up my nerve to talk to the boy I used to watch playing baseball in the park. I wanted her to know that I'm still connected to him. And there's another boy . . . I don't know where he is, but I know somehow I'm connected to him, too.

I know I'll probably never see Brent again, and Rob and I can't go back to holding hands in the park. But that day I rode the subway for a long time and thought about everything that had happened. And I finally figured out one thing.

It's about those good books. The ones with the sad endings. I used to worry because all the good books had sad endings. But I figured out that I don't need to worry. Because in real life there are no endings.

ABOUT THE AUTHOR

J. Hannah Orden grew up in Chicago, Illinois. She received her bachelor of arts degree in theater from Antioch College, and her masters degree in education from Simmons College in Boston. For many years, her primary interest was in theater, and she has pursued this interest through her work as an actor, director, playwright, and drama teacher. Her first play, *A House Divided*, was produced in the spring of 1988 at the Ironbound Theater in Newark, New Jersey. Ms. Orden's experience as a high school teacher of drama and English inspired her to write *In Real Life*, her first novel for young adults. She and her daughter live in Boston.

PZ 7 .O627 In
Orden, J. Hannah.
In real life

DATE DUE

HORACE W. STURGIS LIBRARY
KENNESAW STATE COLLEGE
MARIETTA, GEORGIA 30061

DEMCO